Sebastian was claiming to be the missing heir to the throne of St. Michel?

Marie-Claire stood in the doorway, not sure that
she'd heard correctly. His words hung in the air.

Why had he never told her this before? And, if he
were the missing heir, wouldn't that make him the
Crown Prince? And, if he were the Crown Prince,
wouldn't that make him Philippe's son, which
would then make him—

Marie-Claire's ears began to buzz. Her face
caught fire and bile rose in her throat. Suddenly,
the enormity of this moment hit her like a ton of
bricks and she felt as though she would faint.

But it was her heart that refused to believe what he
was saying. Because with the feelings she had for
Sebastian LeMarc, there was no way he could be
her brother....

* * *

Don't miss next month's installment of
ROYALLY WED: THE MISSING HEIR—
In Pursuit of a Princess
by Donna Clayton (SR #1582)

Dear Reader,

Calling all royal watchers! This month, Silhouette Romance's Carolyn Zane kicks off our exciting new series, ROYALLY WED: THE MISSING HEIR, with the gem *Of Royal Blood*. Fans of last year's ROYALLY WED series will love this thrilling four-book adventure, filled with twists and turns—and of course, plenty of love and romance. Blue bloods and commoners alike will also enjoy Laurey Bright's newest addition to her VIRGIN BRIDES thematic series, *The Heiress Bride*, about a woman who agrees to marry to protect the empire that is rightfully hers.

This month is also filled with earth-shattering secrets! First, award-winning author Sharon De Vita serves up a whopper in her latest SADDLE FALLS title, *Anything for Her Family*. Natalie McMahon is much more than the twin boys' nanny—she's their mother! And in Karen Rose Smith's *A Husband in Her Eyes*, the heroine has her eyesight restored, only to have haunting visions of a man and child. Can she bring love and happiness back into their lives?

Everyone likes surprises, right? Well, in Susan Meier's *Married Right Away*, the heroine certainly gives her boss the shock of his life—she's having his baby! And Love Inspired author Cynthia Rutledge makes her Silhouette Romance debut with her modern-day Cinderella story, *Trish's Not-So-Little Secret*, about "Fatty Patty" who comes back to her hometown a beautiful swan—and a single mom with a jaw-dropping secret!

We hope this month that you feel like a princess and enjoy the royal treats we have for you from Silhouette Romance.

Happy reading!

Mary-Theresa Hussey

Mary-Theresa Hussey
Senior Editor

Please address questions and book requests to:
Silhouette Reader Service
U.S.: 3010 Walden Ave., P.O. Box 1325, Buffalo, NY 14269
Canadian: P.O. Box 609, Fort Erie, Ont. L2A 5X3

Of Royal Blood

CAROLYN ZANE

SILHOUETTE *Romance*®
Published by Silhouette Books
America's Publisher of Contemporary Romance

Special thanks and acknowledgment
are given to Carolyn Zane for her contribution to the
ROYALLY WED: THE MISSING HEIR series.

For Rita Dubenko, neighbor, friend,
one dang fast race-walker, and sister-friend
of whom it is said, "She is faithful."

Thanks to You, Lord, for Your amazing faithfulness.

Do not be afraid of sudden terror,
nor of trouble from the wicked when it comes.
For the Lord will be your confidence.
—Proverbs 3:25-26

SILHOUETTE BOOKS

ISBN 0-373-19576-1

OF ROYAL BLOOD

Visit Silhouette at www.eHarlequin.com

Printed in U.S.A.

Books by Carolyn Zane

Silhouette Romance

The Wife Next Door #1011
Wife in Name Only #1035
*Unwilling Wife #1063
*Weekend Wife #1082
Bachelor Blues #1093
The Baby Factor #1127
Marriage in a Bottle #1170
It's Raining Grooms #1205
†Miss Prim's Untamable
   Cowboy #1248
†His Brother's Intended Bride #1266
†Cinderella's Secret Baby #1308
†The Rich Gal's Rented Groom #1339
†Johnny's Pregnant Bride #1402
†The Millionaire's Waitress Wife #1482
†Montana's Feisty Cowgirl #1488
†Tex's Exasperating Heiress #1494
Of Royal Blood #1576

*Sister Switch
†The Brubaker Brides

Yours Truly

Single in Seattle
How To Hook a Husband
   (and a Baby)

Silhouette Books

The Coltons: Brides of Privilege
"Destiny's Bride"

The Coltons
Taking On Twins

CAROLYN ZANE

lives with her husband, Matt, their preschool daughter Madeline and their latest addition, baby daughter Olivia, in the rolling countryside near Portland, Oregon's Willamette River. Like Chevy Chase's character in the movie *Funny Farm*, Carolyn finally decided to trade in a decade of city dwelling and producing local television commercials for the quaint country life of a novelist. And even though they have bitten off decidedly more than they can chew in the remodeling of their hundred-plus-year-old farmhouse, life is somewhat saner for her than for poor Chevy. The neighbors are friendly, the mail carrier actually stops at the box and the dog, Bob Barker, sticks close to home.

THE DE BERGERONS OF ST. MICHEL

King Antoine de Bergeron (d)
m.
Queen Simone

King Philippe

1st marriage
Katie Graham (d)

The Missing Heir?
A Prince at Last, SR #1594, 6/02

2nd marriage
Johanna Van Rhys (D)

Lise
A Princess in Waiting, SR #1588, 5/02

Ariane
In Pursuit of a Princess, SR #1582, 4/02

MARIE-CLAIRE m. SEBASTIAN LeMARC
Of Royal Blood, SR #1576, 3/02

3rd marriage
Helene Beaudreau (d)

Georges
Juliet

Jacqueline

4th marriage
Celeste Buscari

Unborn Child

Key:
d Deceased
D Divorced
= Child from previous marriage

Chapter One

Princess Marie-Claire de Bergeron—third daughter of Philippe de Bergeron, king of St. Michel, a small nation just north of France—squeezed between her two older sisters in order to better view the amazing physique of Sebastian LeMarc: playboy, aristocrat, successful import/export trade businessman. Clutching her sisters' arms to keep from falling too far back in the crowd, she watched with rapt fascination as he paused in his approach to the seventeenth hole to sign an autograph for a giggly young fan.

In St. Michel, Sebastian was a local celebrity. A good-natured philanthropist, a sex symbol and an all around hotty.

"Hotty, hot-hot," Marie-Claire murmured, loving faddish American slang nearly as much as she loved American movies, TV and cheeseburgers.

"Get away, Marie-Claire." Her oldest sister, the newly married Lise batted at her. "You are breathing down my neck."

Obligingly, Marie-Claire popped up over her middle sister, Ariane's, shoulder and allowed her gaze to follow the handsome Sebastian as he signaled his caddie.

In homes all over the globe, golf enthusiasts followed this action on a cable sports channel. Color and comment announcers strained toward a bank of television monitors and murmured, "He's approaching the tee…uh-oh." Muffled laughter.

"We seem to have a bit of a problem on the course. Sebastian LeMarc's caddie has taken a spill."

"That's right, Frank. Looks like it'll be a minute."

"From what we are able to gather here in the press box, LeMarc's regular caddie was under the weather…"

"Too much celebration after yesterday's rounds?"

More male laughter. Papers rustled.

"Rob, the caddie pinch-hitting for LeMarc today is, believe it or not, the son of the de Bergeron palace gardener, eighteen-year-old Eduardo Van Groober from St. Michel. Eduardo was on his high school's golf team last year and hopes one day to be the next Tiger Woods."

"Let's see if he can stay on his feet."

More chuckling.

"I think he was distracted."

"The king's daughters would do that to the most seasoned caddie, I'm afraid."

On television, cutaways of Marie-Claire and her attractive sisters filled the screen.

Marie-Claire watched as the flame-faced Eduardo fumbled with the golf bag, rushing to insert the clubs and frantically searching for one to offer Sebastian.

Sebastian found a club lying on the ground and, stepping over the still-flailing Eduardo, moved to the tee.

"Frank, Sebastian LeMarc looks to be using a seven iron, an excellent choice. With his powerful swing and ability to focus, this next shot could put his team in the lead."

Marie-Claire wriggled with excitement, but when a thoughtless member of the press obscured her view, she dropped down and poked her head under Lise's elbow, only to receive a glare of exasperation for her effort.

"Stop skulking around beneath us, Marie-Claire," Lise admonished in low tones. "Your hair is so filled with static, you look as if you've been electrocuted."

I feel that way, Marie-Claire thought, catching an exhilarating glimpse of her hero from between the reporter's lanky legs as Sebastian took a few practice swings.

"Ouch! What in heaven's name are you doing?" Ariane demanded as Marie-Claire's knees found the tips of her toes.

"Trying to see…him."

Ariane guffawed. "He's got to be what, twenty-eight? Twenty-nine?"

"Thirty-two."

"*Mon Dieu!* You're too young for him."

"I am not."

"Are too. Just look at you now."

"He's noticed me before."

Lise and Ariane exchanged droll glances. "When?"

Marie-Claire considered silence but their expressions spurred her to divulge. "It began five years ago. When I was sixteen, and we had a…moment."

"A…moment?" Lise asked.

"*Sixteen?* You are hallucinating." Ariane smirked.

"No. He remembers me, I know it."

"What kind of moment? Did you run over him in driver's training?" Pretty heads together, Lise and Ariane hooted. Marie-Claire pulled herself to her feet and, eyes blazing, attempted to tame her flyaway hair.

"He knows who I *am,* I tell you."

"He *knows* all of Papa's offspring."

"That's not what I mean. This is a special connection. You wouldn't understand."

Ariane snorted. "Marie-Claire, you are such a dreamer."

"Be that as it may, he carries a tiny place in his heart just for me." Marie-Claire turned her back on her skeptical sisters and focused on Sebastian, who in that moment, turned, caught her eye, and shot her a sexy wink. "See? Did you see that?" Her voice a tinny squeak, she yanked on her sisters' arms. "He winked at me!"

Lise lifted her nose. "He was not winking at you. The sun was merely in his eyes."

"The sun is *behind* his head!"

Ariane had to give her that. "Then he winks at all the pesky little kids in the kingdom. See? He just winked at Eduardo."

"And," Lise pointed out, "if I'm not mistaken, Eduardo just winked at you, Marie-Claire."

"He wants you, Marie-Claire." Ariane laughed.

"Shut up."

"Marie-Claire Van Groober. That's very pretty, don't you think?" Lise and Ariane made slobbery smooching sounds and then snickered into their hands.

Marie-Claire decided to ignore them.

Sebastian...*LeMarc*.

Marie-Claire *LeMarc*. Mentally, she traced the letters of his surname in her mind. For five long years he'd starred in her fantasy life, playing the part of her future husband and the father of their four yet-to-be-conceived children, three sons and a beautiful daughter.

Oh, that he would only notice her again, the way he had that night. She flushed, as those memories came flooding back. She knew he remembered. He must. How could he forget?

As he surveyed the fairway, she studied the confident curl

of amusement that seemed so permanently etched in his upper lip. She took in the slightly cynical, yet thoroughly charming creases that bracketed the corners of his mouth. The thick, dark-brown hair with the tiniest smattering of silver at the temples. The squarish, masculine chin that sported an angel's thumbprint. The velvety midnight-blue eyes and the come-hither look he seemed completely unaware he exuded from beneath the thick fringe of his lashes. Somehow, he looked more like George Clooney than George Clooney.

All around her, women were salivating, posing to attract his attention, applying lipstick and nudging each other. Marie-Claire's shoulders flagged. Her sisters were right. He had no time for her. Sebastian was an experienced, sophisticated man. And she? Well, at twenty-one, she was surely an overly sheltered case of arrested development. It was hard to become an independent, worldly wise woman with bodyguards and security cameras monitoring her every move.

Wildflowers need air. Light.

Hunkering low, Sebastian peered down his club, a thoughtful expression on his boyish mug. With a nod and a last murmured confab with Marie-Claire's father, King Philippe, he stood, pressed his tee into the grass and set his ball atop. Carefully, he positioned his feet and squinted once again down the fairway.

Oh, this was so exciting. Even the back of his head was enthralling. Sebastian was about to bring her father's team to certain victory.

Marie-Claire strained forward, knocking Ariane off-balance.

A hush descended over the crowd.

Sebastian laced his fingers over the handle of the club and, having lined up his shot, drew back.

On the down swing the words *"Go, Sebastian!"* pierced the hush and too late, Marie-Claire realized that the giddy shriek had come from the depths of her own throat. She wanted to die.

People turned to stare.

King Philippe rolled his eyes.

Buck teeth poking through his smile, Eduardo shot her the thumbs-up.

Her sisters' strangled giggles revealed their horror. Lise hissed, "You're not supposed to yell at a golf tournament, you silly twit, have you lost your mind?"

Ears still ringing, Ariane gawped at her. "It's no wonder he's noticed you. You're a loon."

Much to his credit, Sebastian managed to execute a perfect shot, straight down the fairway, ending up a mere yard from the flag. The crowd went wild. Grins broad, King Philippe and Sebastian locked their hands overhead in a victory high-five and the paparazzi went nuts, scribbling on their pads, cameras flashing.

Through the throng, Marie-Claire felt Sebastian's eyes search her out as he turned and, once again, winked at her. Hands to face, her cheeks scalded the cool tips of her fingers and, in spite of her mortification, she smiled.

Their gazes met and clung, as they had, from time to time, over the years.

Around them, noises and colors swirled. Reality fell away. Marie-Claire's heart skipped several important beats and planet Earth seemed suddenly to be rotating backwards, so slowly was everything moving.

Sunlight glinted off the back of Sebastian's head, highlighting his dark hair in a glorious crown of burnished gold. He dipped his regal chin, his deep bedroom eyes never leaving hers and he arched a brow so loaded with questions that Marie-Claire knew.

He remembered.

* * *

Now that the tournament had ended, people were headed home to get ready for the victory celebration being held at the de Bergeron Palace that evening. A great ocean of humanity flowed past the clubhouse to the parking lot and gridlock was immediate. Impatient horns sounded and threatening shouts only added to the festive feel of victory.

Sebastian LeMarc watched his caddie as the lanky, flame-haired Van Groober lad stood staring after Marie-Claire. His freckled face wore the twitter-pated look of unrequited love. Sebastian knew the feeling. He'd been watching the stunning Marie-Claire de Bergeron from afar for half a decade now. Along with most of the male population of St. Michel.

But that was going to change.

Tonight.

She was twenty-one. Fully grown and fair game. And he had a good feeling that his interest was reciprocated. At least he hoped so. She was an amazing young woman. Full of vitality and as beautiful on the inside as she was on the outside.

Apparently, Eduardo thought so, too.

"She's something, huh, man?" Sebastian clapped the gangly lad on the back.

"Yes, sir. I mean no, sir! I'm not...I could never..." He tore his gaze from Marie-Claire's retreating form and stared up at Sebastian. "Have you ever been in love, Mr. Le-Marc?"

Sebastian took his golf bag from the skinny Van Groober and shouldered it with an easy move. "Yes."

"What happened?"

"Nothing." He squinted off into the throng. "Yet."

From where she stood in her suite behind the king's state apartment, Marie-Claire could hear the muted strains of a victory party gearing up from the grand Crystal Ballroom below. She pressed her nose to a balcony window to better see the headlights swinging around the circular drive at the front of the castle to the valet parking area.

For the umpteenth time, she wondered when *he* would arrive. She strained to make out his sleek Peugeot through the gloaming and almost thought she saw it parked in the family's private guest area. No doubt he was already downstairs, mingling. Though there were slated to be somewhere between twelve- and fifteen-hundred guests, for Marie-Claire, there was only one.

Sebastian LeMarc.

Light-headed with anticipation, Marie-Claire pushed the window ajar and music wafted in on the evening breeze. Every window in the palace blazed, and the gardens that unfurled from its rock walls were strategically lit to invite the fairy Queen Mab's dreamers, or young lovers in clandestine escape.

It was unusually warm for the first week in September, sultry, deceptively lazy, for the humidity lent an electric quality to the air, almost as if the thunderclouds looming in the distance might roll by and let loose with a wild abandon that would rival the emotional storm brewing beneath her breast.

Palms to the ornately carved window casing, she levered herself from her fascination with the arriving guests and moved to her vanity to give her gown a tentative twirl and to check her makeup one last time for flaws. After a breathless inspection, she deemed herself to be as ready as she'd ever be, and set off to find her sisters.

"How do I look?" Marie-Claire burst into Ariane's suite to find her helping Lise fasten a dazzling choker of platinum, gold and diamond baguettes about her neck. No doubt a gift from Wilhelm Rodin, Lise's husband of less than a month. Appearances were important to Wilhelm.

They both spared Marie-Claire a casual glance.

"You look quite grown up this evening," Ariane allowed. "Hoping to catch Sebastian in a weak moment and club him over the head and drag him by the hair to your cave?"

Fingers to lips, Lise pinched back her amusement.

"Yes, as a matter of fact, I am." With a grin, Marie-Claire waved off the sisterly jibe. "Any advice?"

Lise sobered. "Yes. Stay away from men."

"This from a newlywed?" Marie-Claire's own smile faded and she exchanged a concerned glance with Ariane.

"Wilhelm and I were never a love match, you know that."

"Yes, but we thought you were at the least very good friends."

Lise shrugged. "They say that even for lovers, the first year is the hardest. For friends, I imagine it to be…less appealing."

Marie-Claire ached for her sister. She could never imagine agreeing to a marriage of convenience. It was lucky Papa hadn't chosen her to create a political alliance between St. Michel and Rhineland because, though Wilhelm was handsome and charming, there was no warmth in the depths of his velvety brown eyes.

Not at all like the sexy twinkle that sparked in Sebastian's eyes when he caught her gaze and held it across a crowded room. Marie-Claire gave her head a slight shake. She would ponder Lise's marriage another time. Tonight, she had a date with destiny.

To Ariane, "What from you, dear sister? Any words to impart, to aid me in my mission?"

Ariane sighed. "Quite simply? Stay off the floor, *try* to

keep your hair pinned neatly to your head, and check your teeth for spinach, if you must eat. Speak when spoken to, and don't, under any circumstances, let on that you care. Play it cool. Men like that.''

Marie-Claire frowned. They *did?*

Always the practical one, Ariane had little time for whimsy.

But Marie-Claire was a much freer spirit. ''I'm off.''

''But we're not ready.''

''So?''

''You're surely not thinking of descending the stair by yourself?''

''Oh, pish, Lise. This is the new millennium. You don't have to do everything you are told to do, you know.'' Marie-Claire moved to the heavy double doors and swished through to the hall. ''Don't dally, or you'll miss all the fun.''

As Sebastian LeMarc watched Marie-Claire descend the grand staircase into the spectacular Crystal Ballroom— named for the priceless one-of-a-kind set of Austrian crystal chandeliers that shimmered fire the full length of the ceiling—he was transported back five years, to a night not unlike this.

His eyes caught hers and held and the age-old tightening kindled within his gut. Just as it had every time he'd caught her eye for the last five years.

Yes, it had been a night very much like this indeed. The second of September, to be exact. The air had been heavy that day, too. Muggy. Thunderclouds threatened harmlessly on the horizon, omitting an occasional distant rumble. The trees were only just beginning to turn into what would soon be a kaleidoscope of lemon-yellows, burnished golds, rusty oranges, and blood-reds.

It was that hour of the day just before the sun fell off its tentative perch on yonder hilltops and cast an ethereal glow over the land, turning raindrops to diamonds and ordinary leaves into a vibrant, translucent mass of color that would rival any pirate's treasure trove. Against the charcoal gray of the dramatic sky these colors came to life in a way that only the most talented old masters had been able to replicate on canvas.

Sebastian had been out riding with friends when he reined in his mount in order to bask in the glory of this magic view. His friends—royal consorts and visiting dignitaries deep in a political discussion—hadn't bothered to look up and rode on ahead for the palace stables.

The air held anticipation.

But of what? Sebastian couldn't pinpoint the source of the restlessness he felt burning deep in his gut. Perhaps it was the changing of the seasons. Or, the melancholia of saying goodbye to another warm sunny time of year and heading inside to spend months beside the fire.

Then again, perhaps it was the feeling that in three short years he'd be thirty. An age when people began to look toward producing a legacy of some sort. A marriage. An heir. To contribute to society in ways other than hunting with the boys and making the aristocratic social scene that had been handed him at birth.

For a long moment, Sebastian sat on his mount and pondered his universe as the sun began its nightly descent behind distant hills and the shadows grew long.

And then, just as he was about to turn homeward for the night, a blinding streak shot out of one of the royal stables farthest from the main compound. With a gleeful war whoop, this shrieking banshee took off across the meadow on a horse—or a bolt of lightning, Sebastian couldn't be sure—and headed toward the woods nearly a kilometer away from the rear of the stables.

Sebastian squinted into the setting sun. Where would a stable boy be charging off to at this hour? Unless he was up to no good.

Reining his horse around, Sebastian set off after the boy, knowing that King Philippe would never have sanctioned such after-hours escapades. The quickest way to ruin prime horseflesh was to ride at breakneck speeds in the dusk.

The wind whistled in his ears as he hunched low and followed the boy over the rolling hills of St. Michel to the edge of a great forest that was rumored still to harbor a fire-breathing dragon and a band of magical fairies. Well, Sebastian didn't know about that, but when he caught up with this kid, be might just breathe a little fire himself.

Upon reaching the forest, he had to slow dramatically to pick his way through the trees to avoid being clothes-lined by a low-lying branch. He could hear the horse and rider just ahead, crashing through the underbrush, and then the roar of falling water as a rushing river cascaded over a precipice at one end of the king's well-stocked fishing pond.

A poacher, no doubt. There to catch a few illegal fish for his undoubtedly lazy, thieving family. Jaw grim with determination, Sebastian stayed just far enough behind to keep this unsavory character in view, while at the same time taking care to avoid being detected. Slowly now, he wove amongst the dense foliage. It was darker deep in the woods, growing more so as the sun's rays began to fade.

Overhead, the sky rumbled an ominous growl, and Sebastian felt the first of several warm drops splat on his head and hands. Urging his mount forward, he peered through the branches and was instantly rewarded with a view that stole his breath away.

This was no boy, standing on an outcropping of rock, hastily shedding his clothes.

No.

This was a young woman!

Casually grazing, her horse was tethered to a tree near the water's edge, about a dozen or so feet beneath the spot where she stood silhouetted against a fiery backdrop of fir trees. Lit from behind as she was by the sun, dusty rays fanned out in a long star pattern as she moved, giving her an almost wraithlike appearance.

Unable to tear his eyes away, he watched as she snatched open her buttons and pulled her blouse free of her jeans. Next, she yanked down the zipper of her pants and eased them over her slender hips. An impatient kick sent them into a haphazard pile with her blouse to the shore below.

Clad in only a pair of lacy wisps that left little to the imagination, she stood and surveyed the way the setting sun shimmered like gold coins bobbing on the surface of the gently lapping waves.

Sebastian's breathing grew shallow. Who was this woman? She was no stable hand, this he knew, as females were never hired in such a capacity in this particular kingdom.

Her body was long and lithesome, yet curvy in all the right spots. Her thighs and calves were shapely, well muscled obviously from years spent riding, and her shoulderlength hair was wild, glowing gold with the slanting light of the setting sun.

Sebastian's mouth went dry. He knew he probably had no business standing there, staring at her this way, when she thought she was by herself, but on the other hand, she had no business being out here alone. It wasn't safe. Anything could happen to a young woman out swimming after dark.

Deciding to stay put, just in case she needed him for whatever reason, he watched as she moved to the edge of the outcropping of rock and surveyed the black water below. As if in slow motion, she balanced on her toes, crouched low, and then using the rock as a springboard, arched out over the water and executed a perfect, nearly splashless, dive.

Sebastian felt as if he'd swallowed a golf ball whole as he watched her disappear from view. When the water's ripples had calmed, his guts began to churn. Where the devil was she? She should have been up already.

He stood in his stirrups and craned in her direction, mentally preparing to go in after her. He waited another three or four seconds.

That did it.

She was in trouble. Likely hit a rock, or maybe she was caught by the hair on some branch beneath the surface of the water.

Throwing a leg over his saddle, he dismounted and hit the ground running in one fluid move. Just as he reached the edge of the pond, she burst forth from the water's surface, like a phoenix rising, her giddy laughter ringing out as she whipped her bra and panties in a circle over her head and flung them onto the beach.

Sebastian could only stand there and stare. His heart was beating ninety miles an hour and the battle he waged was whether to paddle this brat for scaring him so, or to kiss her because she was alive.

And beautiful.

In his life, the plastic, well-bred beauties that vied for his attention had jaded Sebastian. Aristocratic women could be so dull. Vain. In search of a trophy to call husband.

But this woman was different, he could tell. Her complete lack of affectation captivated him, and he found himself wanting to know more. Was she a commoner? If so, who was her father? What did he do?

Then reality struck.

Could she be taken? She certainly did not act the staid,

married matron. Her body and her carefree personality betrayed her youth and he judged her to be no more than twenty. Twenty-two at the most.

A perfect complement to his twenty-seven.

Watching her, he felt his world-weary cares begin to seep away. There was something mysterious about this mermaid. She inspired ridiculous thoughts. Flights of fancy he'd given up entertaining long ago. Thoughts of the magic of finding one's true love.

His heart began to pound and his blood rushed powerfully through his body. He flexed his hands, and watched her move to stand waist-deep at the opposite shore, her back toward him, wet hair tickling her shoulder blades. Hands cupped, she used them as a scoop to douse stray tendrils away from her face.

Then, as if she suddenly sensed that she wasn't alone, the woman slowly turned to face him, her arms snaking across her bare breasts just before she sank to her shoulders in the water.

"Who is there?" she demanded.

Sebastian stepped forward and their eyes locked for an infinite, supercharged moment before he spoke.

"Perhaps I should be asking you the same question, woman. This is the private property of His Royal Highness, King Philippe. You are breaking the law by stealing one of his horses and swimming in his pond after dark."

The woman did not seem daunted, and instead smiled. "I'm not afraid of him."

"Then perhaps you'd consider being afraid of me."

"And who, pray tell, are you?"

"I am Sebastian LeMarc, a friend of the royal family and, when I have to be, the nude-beach police. Who are you?"

She tossed back her head and sent throaty laughter into

the twilight. "You know, Sebastian LeMarc, you should probably join me. To cool that hot head of yours."

Sebastian stared at this cheeky sprite. Who the devil did she think she was? "If I have to, I'll come in there after you."

"Suit yourself. Or not. This is a suit-optional pool." She giggled, tickled with herself, and Sebastian couldn't help but smile as she dove beneath the water's surface, sending a spray of drops into the air.

What was he going to do with this woman? Dragging a slippery porpoise, one that had no intention of being caught no less, out of the water would be a challenge indeed.

She surfaced, this time nearer the waterfall and beckoned to him. "Come on in. The water's fine."

"Didn't your parents ever tell you not to play naked with strangers?"

She laughed. "Yes. But you are not a stranger."

"You know my name only."

"I know that my father trusts you."

"And who would your father be?"

"You really don't know?"

"If I did, would I have to ask?"

"I am the third daughter of Philippe de Bergeron, King of St. Michel, and owner of this pond."

Sebastian stared, mouth agape. That was impossible. Marie-Claire de Bergeron was a child! He wracked his brain, attempting to recall her age, but she was certainly no more than twelve or thirteen. He'd never given the king's young daughters a second thought, as over the years they seemed more occupied with the affairs of dolls and roller skates than with affairs of state. On the odd social occasion that he'd come in contact with the king's children, he'd been preoccupied. Concerned with the well-being of his date du jour, or the hour's political topic.

Languidly, she swam toward the beach where he stood and finding purchase on a submerged rock with her toes, allowed her shoulders to protrude from the water.

His eyes dipped to the cleavage she cradled in her arms. Seems he'd lost track of her birthdays. Suddenly guilty at the lascivious direction his thoughts had taken, he took a giant step back.

"Does your father know you are here?"

"Papa is too busy to keep track of me."

"Every father wants to know that his children are safe. Especially after dark."

"I am no longer a child," she argued hotly. "As of yesterday, I am sixteen years old. A royal debutante, of an age to begin dating."

Sebastian snorted, even as a keen disappointment settled in his gut. *Sixteen?* She was a child. "You are a royal pain, of an age to be spanked and I'm tempted to be the one to do it. Get out of the water now."

"Make me."

Sebastian arched a brow. "You are a brat."

"And you are a killjoy."

She aroused myriad emotions within him, and his jaw flexed as he pondered his next move. It was rare that anyone, let alone a teenaged girl, challenged his authority. And strangely, it exhilarated him.

For the longest moment, neither of them spoke. The only sounds were those of the rushing waterfall and the soulful cadence of the cricket's song. Somewhere in the distance, an owl hooted. The sun disappeared altogether, leaving the storm clouds on the horizon, silver-plated. The steady *plip-plop* of raindrops turned into an all-out shower, but still neither of them moved. Nor spoke.

At least, not with words.

Even so, they knew that what was passing between them

was life-changing, for them both. He waged a battle in his mind, but was far too ethical to take advantage of her foolishness.

You're too young.

But I won't always be.

I'll wait.

Do.

With a nod, Sebastian turned and easily mounted his horse and set off through the trees.

''Get dressed,'' he ordered over his shoulder. ''I'll wait for you at the edge of the woods and escort you safely home.''

This time, she did not argue.

Chapter Two

She'd turned twenty-one just yesterday. This Sebastian knew, as he'd etched the date on his brain five long years ago. And now, as the beautiful Marie-Claire de Bergeron descended the stair alone, all eyes in the steadily growing crowd turned to greet this vision with approval and, he noted with a swift glance about, some lechery.

A fierce wave of protectiveness washed over him and he excused himself from a conversation he was having with Lise's new husband, Wilhelm Rodin, and moved to stand at the bottom of the stairs.

As it had so often in the past, his gaze drew hers and they were locked in a world of their own making. Only now, they both knew she was a full-fledged adult, legal in every way and responsible for her own decisions in this life.

Seeming to sense the moment was perfect, the royal orchestra struck up a rousing waltz and Sebastian held his hand out to Marie-Claire.

"Dance?"

"*Oui.*"

Bashfully, she extended her hand and he suppressed the grin he felt surging up from his belly. She was such a conundrum. One minute, she was wildly cheering him to victory on the golf course and the next, a blushing innocent, struggling to exude sophistication. Though soft and small, her hand was strong, and she clung to him as he led her through the throng to the dance floor.

When they arrived, a number of couples were already sweeping about the gleaming marble. King Philippe danced with his wife, Queen Celeste; Philippe's mother, the Dowager Queen Simone danced with the prime minister, Rene Davoine; and a number of court consorts, celebrities and political acquaintances from different countries also whirled across the Russian imported flooring.

Sebastian drew Marie-Claire's lithe body against his own and it was like a homecoming. He breathed in the scent of her perfumed hair and rested his hand at the small dip in her lower back. Holding her this way was far more exhilarating than any dream he'd ever had. As he'd known they would, they fitted as if they were born to be together.

Shyly, she glanced up at him, and it was the first time ever he'd seen her at such close range. Her skin was the flawless stuff of youth, peachy smooth and the color of cream with a hint of cinnamon. Tonight, her sun-streaked hair was upswept, revealing the graceful length of her neck, and her almond-shaped eyes reflected the emerald sheen of the satin confection she wore. Shadowed by the ghost of a smile, her lips were slightly parted and Sebastian longed to press his mouth to them, to see if their kiss would be as explosive as he'd imagined over the years.

However, this was not the time or place for such a first. He wanted it to be perfect. And he wanted them to be alone. For now, he would settle for the joy of simply holding her in his arms. That, and the knowledge that he was the luckiest man in the room.

"Your twenty-first birthday was yesterday, no?"

Marie-Claire's gaze shot to his. "How did you know?"

"Math."

"Math?" Her smile was quizzical.

"On this day, five years ago, you had been sixteen for a whole day."

A charming flush crawled up her slender neck and settled in her cheeks. "You remember that day?"

"Vaguely." Someday, when they'd been long married, he'd confess how the memory had plagued him, ruining subsequent relationships and making sport of his sleep. "Happy Birthday."

"Thank you."

"What did you do to celebrate this time?"

"For one thing, I stayed out of the pond."

"Too bad."

Again, the endearing blush. "Papa took me to Paris for the day. I went shopping for this gown."

"Excellent choice."

"You think so?"

"Mmm. I think you are easily the most beautiful cheerleader in the room."

Marie-Claire heaved a heavy sigh and stared down at the floor. "So you heard that?"

Unable to restrain the grin that tugged at his lips, Sebastian ducked his head so that he could peer into her face. "Marie-Claire, thanks to the wonders of cable television, the entire world heard that."

"How singularly mortifying."

"I thought it was charming. Cute."

"Cute?" She made a face. "Now everyone thinks I have a schoolgirl crush on you."

He tipped her chin, forcing her gaze to meet his. "And do you?"

Suddenly seeming to forget her mission to prove herself the sedate lady, her candid laughter had his pulse surging.

"Well, since the entire world knows, I suppose there is no point in lying to you. I guess you could say I have an…infatuation, where you're concerned. But…" she held up a finger, smiled brightly and blathered on, "I'm struggling to overcome that. I'm thinking of joining a twelve-step program. Not that I'm a stalker or anything—"

"Don't do that on my account."

"What?"

"Don't abandon your…addiction."

She stumbled over his foot. "No?"

"No."

"Oh." She stared up at him and smiled.

He smiled back, and her heart took wing. This moment was perfect. The musical medley picked up pace and segued into a driving rumba. Marie-Claire loved to rumba.

"May I cut in?"

Marie-Claire froze.

Eduardo, his teeth pointing at Marie-Claire from behind his eager smile, tapped Sebastian on the shoulder. His wild, rusty head of hair had been tamed with what looked like an entire bottle of styling gel and his tuxedo was inches too short in the sleeve and cuff. Fingers itching, he fairly pried Marie-Claire from Sebastian's grasp.

She wanted to scream as Sebastian stepped aside and with obvious reluctance handed her over to the young Eduardo Van Groober's arms. Darn! Just as things were getting interesting. Eduardo clutched her close and her back already ached from the pressure he exerted.

"Save another dance for me?" Sebastian called as Eduardo jerked her away, rattling her teeth in the process.

Marie-Claire nodded dumbly and watched with longing as Sebastian backed across the room and straight into the voluptuous—and morally emancipated—Baroness Veronike Schroeder of Germany.

Before Sebastian had time to react, Veronike cast out her web, snared him, and then dragged him out to the dance floor for the kill.

Eduardo made an awkward attempt at conversation and Marie-Claire listened with half an ear. And, when he wasn't trying to impress her with his prowess on the high-school golf team, his nose was buried in her hair. Marie-Claire batted at him in a distracted fashion, straining to keep her sights on Sebastian.

And Veronike.

Euro-trash with pretensions to the Hapsburg dynasty, Veronike was a formidable personality and when she wanted something, she usually got it. And Veronike did enjoy the occasional dalliance with a handsome playboy.

Jealousy seared like a hot knife through Marie-Claire's heart. Compared to Veronike, Marie-Claire felt quite the underdeveloped adolescent. Insecurity assailed her as she watched Veronike swivel seductively to the pounding beat. Veronike draped over Sebastian like a skimpy chiffon window dressing, all fluttering lashes and fat, blood-red lips.

The dress the German siren wore tonight seemed less a gown and more a figment of the imagination. Smashed against Sebastian's firm chest, Veronike's ample bosom strained to be set free of its wispy confines and her hips ground against Sebastian's in a way that would have Marie-Claire's molars reduced to dust before the end of the evening if she didn't make a concerted effort to change her train of thought.

Ooo.

Wilhelm tapped Eduardo on the shoulder and cut in, no

doubt feeling it was time to put in the appearance of caring, Marie-Claire thought churlishly. Eduardo obviously hated to let her go and there was an awkward scuffle as Wilhelm dismissed the hormone-ravaged boy. Where Eduardo was chatty, Wilhelm was stony, allowing Marie-Claire to drift.

She winced as she retraced the inane conversation she'd made just now with Sebastian, and wondered if she wasn't better off eating her heart out over Veronike's physical charms.

I'm joining a twelve-step program for stalkers.

Her sisters were right. She was certifiable. During her next dance with Sebastian, she hoped—if there *was* a next dance with Sebastian—she'd be able to control her idiotic tongue before she blurted out that she wanted to snatch Veronike bald.

Oh.

Marie-Claire's eyes slid closed as she reflected on how unbelievably right it had felt to have Sebastian's arms around her. She knew he'd felt it, too. She moaned, and an involuntary shiver wracked her body. Head back, she clutched Wilhelm a little tighter at the memory of Sebastian's powerful body steering her around the dance floor. She immediately regretted the impulse as the rigid Wilhelm looked down at her with a curious frown.

"Stiff knee," she fibbed.

After a frightfully dull turn on the dreary Wilhelm's arm, her father at last rescued her, just before Eduardo could reach her again. The boy's disappointment was plain.

"You are looking well tonight, daughter. This gown suits you."

Coming from her father, this was high praise. Though King Philippe was not effusive in speech, Marie-Claire knew she was loved. Cherished. And, because she was the youngest of three daughters by his first—and now deceased—wife a tad favored.

"Thank you, sir. You're looking rather dapper tonight, yourself." She gave his satin cummerbund a playful tug.

"Oh, I know you're simply trying to put a bit of a bounce in an old man's step."

"Fifty-one is hardly old."

"I'm sure it must seem that way when you are just twenty-one. You know, I was Sebastian's age or thereabouts when you were born."

"Oh?"

His smile was gentle. "I see the way you look at him."

"I don't suppose my ladylike caterwauling on the golf course has anything to do with your assumption that I'm smitten."

A chuckle rumbled from deep within Philippe's robust chest, and Marie-Claire couldn't help but notice how handsome her father still was. The little cleft in his chin and the twinkle in his eye put her in mind of another of her favorite American actors, although Michael Douglas was perhaps not quite as tall. But the physical resemblance was something folks had remarked upon before. That and the fact that they both preferred young, beautiful wives.

Marie-Claire spared a glance in Celeste's direction, and noted the raucous laughter and phony social-climbing demeanor her stepmother had assumed with the prime minister. Her father was blind when it came to Celeste's rather lengthy list of foibles.

"I suppose you could do worse than Sebastian." Though Philippe's remark was offhand, as he looked at his daughter, his gaze roved her suddenly burning cheeks.

"Papa!"

He ignored her weak protestations. "You are a beautiful woman, Marie-Claire. Unfortunately for me, the time has

come to let go of you. To let you loose upon the world...."
King Philippe pulled Marie-Claire close, the gesture at odds
with his words.

"Heaven forbid!"

"You will do great things in this life, my dear. Always
know that I love you, and am so very proud."

Marie-Claire felt her throat tighten at his sweet words,
and impulsively stood on her toes to plant a kiss on his
cheek. This pleased the king and he blinked back the tears.

As the evening wore on, Marie-Claire and Sebastian were
obliged to dance with other people. Thankfully, Veronike
was a popular partner and had not been available for a second go at Sebastian. And, though they were not always in
proximity, Marie-Claire could feel Sebastian's proprietary
gaze and her confidence soared. Unable to tear her eyes
away from him for more than a moment, she found keeping
up with the task at hand nearly impossible.

"So," Charles Rodin, Wilhelm's twin brother com-
mented, "I understand you are a fan of old movies. Have
you seen *Adam's Rib*?"

"I have never eaten there, though I do enjoy American
barbecue..."

"Oh?" Charles frowned.

Prince Etienne Kroninberg of Rhineland told her, "It is
my understanding that your sister, Ariane, is planning to
come to my country for a visit."

"No, Ariane is around here somewhere, I think. I just
saw her..."

Etienne opened his mouth as if to speak, then thought
better and shut it.

The prime minister said, "Your grandmother is looking
well tonight. The king's victory seems to have put roses in
her cheeks."

"Yes, she has ten green thumbs, at least."

More than once, she trod upon her partner's toe and had to beg pardon. And more than once, she caught Sebastian's smile of amusement.

After what seemed to be an eternity, Sebastian finally made his way back to her and solicited her hand from a stodgy third cousin and whisked her off.

"Is it hot in here, or is it just me?" Sebastian angled his head and cocked a playful brow.

"I think there is no chaste way to answer that question." Marie-Claire returned his grin.

Admiration for her wit flashed in his eyes. "Shall we set the tongues to wagging and head out to the verandah for a breath of fresh air?"

"Why not? The tongues have been wagging all day."

"Come on then. Let's give them some more grist for the rumor mill."

Marie-Claire's heart bounced about in her rib cage at the intimate quality in his voice.

The verandah outside the ballroom was nearly as large as the ballroom itself. Made of concrete, it sported a low railing with balustrades as broad as small wine kegs. Light poured from the palace windows and the music—a lilting Vivaldi piece—danced upon the gentle night breezes. In the air, there was a hint of burning leaves and the last fragrances of summer's flowers.

Never had Marie-Claire felt more vibrant. Alive. Pulsing with vitality. Sebastian's touch on her hand was warm and this warmth spread up her arm and burned and swirled in her chest, making it hard to catch her breath.

This was the moment she'd been dreaming of. A moment alone with a man with whom she'd bonded, once upon a twilight evening in her youth. And, though before tonight they'd only conversed on the most superficial topics, it was an unbreakable bond, for whatever magical reason. Fate. Kismet.

Destiny.

Didn't matter what one called it. Marie-Claire believed that God himself wanted them together and there was no use even pursuing other options.

A few dried leaves skittered across the patio's floor as a warm wind flirted with Marie-Claire's hair and skirts. A violent shiver wracked her body as anticipation rolled up her spine and settled in her throat.

"Are you cold?"

She swallowed against the excitement that burned in her throat. "No. Quite the opposite, actually."

Sebastian untied his bow tie and unfastened a collar stud with his free hand. "Same."

As they strolled, other couples, seeming to find the climate in the ballroom confining, began to wander out of doors looking for a bit of fresh air and some privacy. Inside the ballroom, Eduardo could be seen, bobbing about, peering out various windows, obviously searching for Marie-Claire.

"Come on."

Sebastian took her hand and tugged her into the shadows and down an immense stair. A sea of rolling lawn unfurled before them, and Marie-Claire bent to remove her high-heeled slippers so that she could better keep up with his rangy stride.

"So. Last time we were alone together, you were sixteen, and of an age to begin dating." He tucked her hand into the crook of his elbow and cast a disarming grin down at her. "Did you?"

"Did I?" Marie-Claire could barely think. The wool of his jacket made a pleasant swooshing sound against the verdant satin of her gown. "What?"

"Date?"

"Oh." How embarrassing. How could she couch the truth and exude the worldly persona she longed for Sebastian to see in her? Her mouth went dry and she touched her tongue to her lips. "Uh... Well, not right away. Actually, Papa caught wind of my plans and shipped me off to an all-girl boarding school."

"I know."

"You knew?"

"I may have inadvertently mentioned your intention to begin dating to him after I escorted you home that night."

Marie-Claire's jaw dropped, and a guttural gasp escaped.

"Apparently, your father was not aware of your plans." Amusement quirked in the corners of Sebastian's lips. "I didn't realize you meant to keep these plans secret."

"Oh, sure." Bristling, she stared at him through narrow eyes. "So. You are the reason I suffered through two years in that horrendously stuffy all-female boarding school?"

"Sorry."

"You should be. The experience was quite scarring."

Sebastian hooted. "I can see that it left you socially retiring."

To keep from being affected by his infectious laughter, she hiked her chin and ignored his teasing tone. "In any event, my dating career had to be postponed until...er... college."

"Ah, but you went to an all-girl college."

Her bravado flagged some. "Don't tell me. All-girl college was your idea, too."

"Of course not." Sebastian shrugged. "I may have had some input but the final decision was always your father's."

Bemused, she stared up at him. How was she ever going to convince him that she was worldly when—thanks in part to him—she'd been cloistered away like a cultured pearl?

Images of Veronike's seductive red lips, puffy and pouty, taunted her and she refused to let him go on thinking of her as some kind of inexperienced virgin.

Even if that's exactly what she was.

"Well, it may have been all girls, but there were men." She wracked her brain for the roster of professors. "There was, um, let's see…Alonzo, and Barnaby and uh, and umm." She frowned. What was his name again? "Cedric! And, uh—"

"An alphabetical accounting of your lovers?"

Her chin jerked up and she could make out the twinkle sparkling in his eyes by the light of the harvest moon. "You don't think I've ever even had a date, do you?" There was a heat in her tone that she struggled to squelch.

"I hope not."

"Oh, you do, do you? Why?"

"Because," he answered simply, as they reached an immense yet shallow reflecting pool, "you're mine."

Marie-Claire was dumbstruck. For a moment, everything went fuzzy, and little pinpricks of light danced before her eyes. Her heart palpitated, and a wild joy sprung from deep within the vicinity of her stomach and, like a flash fire, spread throughout her body.

"Oh." The breathy utterance hovered on the air between them.

"You're not entirely surprised." He paused and turned to face her, lifting her chin with his thumb and forefinger.

"No."

"There is something. It's been there since that night."

"Yes."

"Something special. It's almost as if we were…" He squinted off into the night sky and his Adam's apple bobbed as he searched for the words, "…somehow kindred spirits."

"I know," she whispered.

He dipped his head back toward her and they stood in a shaft of moonlight, regarding each other. Discovering the truth in each other's eyes. It was a powerful moment, fraught with a tension so palpable it generated heat that radiated between their bodies.

Marie-Claire could see that Sebastian was as stunned by the power of their chemistry as she was. For an instant, he seemed to lose his perennial confidence. There was vulnerability in his expression that endeared him impossibly closer to her soul than ever before.

In front of them, seeming to float on the vast surface of the reflecting pool, *Le cheval du roi*—a statue of her great-great grandfather's royal steed—reared, flanked on each side by two equally impressive mares. Years of weather had given the cool, dark metal a streaked green patina. The fountain was especially spectacular when it was lit for a party, as it was tonight.

Seemingly unable to endure the tension that shimmered between them, Sebastian abruptly turned and tugged her to the edge of the pool. He stepped up to the top of the two-foot high wall rim, then helped her up behind him. Off in the distance, strains of an orchestra sounded over the fountain's spray.

Sebastian stepped out of his highly polished wingtips and kicked them to the ground below. Then, reaching for the slippers that dangled from Marie-Claire's fingers, he dropped them on top of his own shoes. "I never did get another dance."

Marie-Claire lifted her arms and draping them over his shoulders, let her wrists dangle. "And so you did not."

"Shall we?"

"We shall."

Marie-Claire whooped in surprise as he took her by the waist and stepped into the pool's knee-deep water. Her gown ballooned on the surface before it sank to swirl about her ankles. Sebastian drew her close and they began to move about their watery dance floor.

Laughing, she leaned away from him so that she could better see his handsome face. This was a moment she would forever remember, she promised herself. Full of hope and possibilities. A veritable dream come to life.

Playfully, he swung her away from him and back again, then bent her low in a dip that had her giddy laughter ringing out. Their spontaneous hilarity caused those who loitered on the verandah to smile with indulgence as the king's youngest daughter frolicked in the fountain with St. Michel's most eligible bachelor. As the tempo of the music increased, so did their silly antics.

Sebastian lifted Marie-Claire in his arms and spun until they were both dizzy and in danger of tipping into the drink.

"You're going to soak us!" Marie-Claire clutched his neck for dear life and wished the ebullient feelings that bubbled into her throat would last forever.

Neither seemed to notice that the music had stopped.

"Don't look now," Sebastian set her down and pulled her up against the solid wall of his chest, "but we're pretty much wet."

Pretending to pout, Marie-Claire leaned sideways. She paused to study her voluminous skirts, hanging heavy against her legs. "I can't go back in now."

"We'd get the floor all wet."

"People might fall."

"You'll let me know if you're thinking of shucking your dress for a skinny dip?" Grin teasing, he cupped her cheek in his palm.

"Will I ever live that night down?"

"You haven't yet. Not in my mind." Their noses grazed as he looked deeply into her eyes. Marie-Claire could feel his warm breath against her lips as he spoke. "Even when you were gone away to school, you were never far from my thoughts."

"I know. It was the same for me."

"You were so young."

"Yes, I was." More than once it had occurred to Marie-Claire that Sebastian could so easily have taken advantage of her foolish crush when she was but a child. But he hadn't. He was an honorable man, and that was only one of the myriad qualities that attracted her. "But I'm not anymore."

"No. You're not." The muscles in his jaw worked as his thoughts seemed to race back over the years. "Waiting for you to grow up has been tedious. I knew any involvement for us before you were of legal age could have caused problems for your father. But—" On a heavy sigh, his eyes slid closed. "For so long, I've wondered…and wanted…."

By now, his lips were brushing hers as he spoke and so it was only a matter of allowing himself to finally indulge in the guilty pleasure of their heretofore forbidden kiss. Ever so slightly, he leaned forward until his lips covered hers in a touch so gossamer, Marie-Claire was tempted to wonder if she was dreaming.

That was all it took for the glowing embers to flare to life.

Immediately, the kiss became heated. Sebastian's arms circled her waist, pulling her closer as his mouth closed over hers. The years of waiting and wondering were over and it was with relief and complete exhilaration that their mouths, their bodies, their souls, came together.

The kiss deepened, and, laboring in sync, their lungs heaved, and their hearts pounded. They struggled to quench their insatiable urge to get closer to each other. To know each other. To learn what they'd wanted to discover for the past five years.

Marie-Claire wound her fingers into the silky soft hair at his nape as he bent to nuzzle her neck and kiss the spot where her shoulder met her neck. A hot blaze shivered down her spine and coiled deep in her belly. In great waves, gooseflesh raced across her body and she gasped at the onslaught. She could hear the thunder of her pulse and wondered how long her heart could take such exertion.

It felt so natural, standing here, being kissed by Sebastian LeMarc. It was as if they had some kind of history together that transcended time. And space. And logic. They were each one half of the other. Whole only when they were together.

And they'd known it that night, five years ago.

Sebastian held Marie-Claire's face in both hands and pulled his mouth away from hers, a fraction. "What are we going to do?"

"Marie-Claire!"

"We've been found out." Sebastian kissed her hard, then took a step back.

Marie-Claire groaned. "My sister, Ariane. Do you think if we ignore her, she'll go away?"

"Likely not. She sounds upset."

Marie-Claire bristled. "I don't know why. I'm old enough to take care of myself. No doubt she saw us and wants to remind me to appear disinterested."

Sebastian grinned. "She's too late."

"We could run," she suggested hopefully.

"Your skirts are too heavy. I'd have to carry you on my back. It would slow me down, but we might stand a chance if we bolt for it now."

Marie-Claire giggled.

"Marie-Claire! *Marie-Claire!* Come quickly! It's *Papa! He's collapsed!*"

Chapter Three

Six months later

It was wonderful to be home.

Marie-Claire had just finished unpacking and moved from her closet to her bedroom window to study the familiar view. It was incredibly warm for March and flowers were blooming early this year. Down below, a veritable army of gardeners swarmed over the de Bergeron Palace's grounds. Mowers roared, clippers hummed and the sweet scent of freshly shorn grass filled the air.

Marie-Claire swallowed against the ever-present lump in her throat. Spring was Papa's favorite time of the year. He'd liked to say it was a time for new beginnings. She stared, unseeing, at the fountain where she and Sebastian had last danced together. She hoped Papa was right. She was finally ready to put the shattered pieces of her life into the dustbin and take a stab at starting over again.

The small country of St. Michel was only just now be-

ginning to recover from the shock of King Philippe's unexpected death. But Marie-Claire doubted that she'd ever
fully mend from the mortal wound to her heart. Her heavy
sigh fogged the windowpane.

Thank God for Sebastian.

During the much-publicized funeral, and in the frenzied
days that followed, he'd been a rock. Though he battled his
own grief—for Philippe had been like a father to him since
Sebastian's own father had passed away when he was a
boy—he was protective and solicitous of Marie-Claire. The
tragedy had only strengthened their special bond and she
loved him more than ever.

Even so, the overwhelming memories of her father
seemed to haunt her healing process. She was an orphan
now. Granted, she was a full-grown orphan, with the money,
power and prestige that came of being born into royalty, but
nonetheless, she felt cut adrift on an ocean of grief. That
she'd been a favorite of her father's only made her anguish
that much more acute.

A deep depression had absconded with Marie-Claire's
usual carefree nature and left her weepy, exhausted and not
caring if she lived or died. She'd known she wouldn't be fit
company for anyone, let alone Sebastian, until she spent
some healing time with her maternal grandmother, Tatiana.
And so, a week after her father was laid to rest and she'd
fulfilled all of her social duties as a member of a grieving
monarchy, Marie-Claire listlessly packed her bags and
headed off to Denmark to find comfort in the bosom of her
mother's side of the family.

The last time she'd seen Sebastian was the day he'd taken
her to the airport and kissed her good-bye. It had been an
emotional kiss, fraught with promises and hope and sorrow
and the terrible knowledge that separation, just as they'd
finally come together, would be hard.

And it had been.

Marie-Claire was sure they could have paid much of St. Michel's national debt with what she and Sebastian had spent in phone charges. But it was worth it to hear his soothing voice. To hear news of home. To know that he still cared.

Tatiana had helped her through the worst of her struggles, talking late into the night, drying her tears, telling her stories of her papa's pride when she'd been born and giving her the benefit of years of living. She was a very wise woman. And for such a tiny thing, she was a tough old broad. Tatiana didn't have time to baby Marie-Claire and after a month, put her to work as a volunteer in a children's hospital in hopes of helping her to see that the rain fell on the just and the unjust.

It worked.

Immediately, Marie-Claire fell in love with the children and in her effort to comfort, was comforted. There was nothing like the sweet feeling of little arms around her neck to soothe her own emotional injuries and before long Marie-Claire had a new life motto and with a gentle push, Tatiana nudged her out of the nest.

"Life is too short to waste even a minute," Marie-Claire murmured against her windowpane. Off in the distance, *Le cheval du roi* came into focus and a sudden burst of happiness that she hadn't felt for half a year filled her breast. "Too short, indeedy." She turned away from the window, rushed to the phone and dialed.

"Hello, Sebastian? I'm home."

Sebastian pocketed his cell phone and, for the first time in ages, his smile was real. Marie-Claire was home. In less than an hour, he'd see her. Hold her. Kiss her. It had been an eternity. These last six months had seemed to drag on longer than the previous five years combined. Yes, waiting for Marie-Claire to grow up had sorely tested his patience, but once he knew the rapture of her kiss, staying away had been hell.

More than once he'd been tempted to barge in on old Tatiana and take what was his, but he knew Marie-Claire needed time. Truth was, he did, too.

Philippe's death had been a shock. Worse, for some reason, than when he'd been a little boy and lost his own father. For as far back as either family could remember, the LeMarcs and the de Bergerons had been close. And Philippe had always been good with Sebastian, possibly seeing him as the son he'd always longed for, Philippe had been a patient mentor, a listening ear, and a model of manliness.

Sebastian missed him. Nearly as much as he'd missed Marie-Claire.

Sebastian reached for his jacket as his mother swept into the over-decorated and cluttered parlor of her sprawling country estate.

"You're leaving? But you just got here." Claudette's face fell as she watched her only son shrug into his jacket and re-knot his tie.

"I'm sorry, Mère. The royal family has requested my presence at lunch today."

"Well, it's about time." Claudette bristled. She gave her short, wavy and, still dark at fifty-two, brown hair a smoothing pat and pursed her lips in dismay at her attire. "This will never do. I'll just be a moment."

"Mère," Sebastian said, suppressing a smile.

Claudette stopped in her tracks and without turning around, heaved a heavy sigh. "I'm not invited. Oh. Well. I see." She waved an airy hand and settled upon a settee as if she had no cares.

But Sebastian could tell she was hurt. Claudette had always been overly enamored with anything that smacked of aristocracy. The fact that she'd been slipping in the St. Michel social ranks since her influential husband had died was not lost on her. A lunch at the palace would surely boost her weight with her cronies down at the club.

"I'm sure it was simply an oversight."

"Of course." Claudette's laughter was brittle. "Why on earth would they invite *you* to lunch over *me?*"

"You see? A simple mistake. I'll give them all your love."

"Yes. Do that, darling. And be sure to tell them how deeply I've been affected by Philippe's death." Making odd faces, Claudette peered into a gilt mirror hanging next to the settee and checked the corners of her eyes and mouth for stray bits of makeup.

"Yes. I'll do that too."

"Good. Well. When can you come back? We barely had a chance to talk and there is something I need to discuss with you."

"What?"

"It's…" Claudette huffed in irritation. "It's financial. I can barely believe it, but I seem to be having some credit problems. I'm sure there must be some mistake down at the bank. Some silly twit or other has punched in the wrong number and left me practically penniless. Could you straighten this out for me?"

"Mère…"

Claudette took immediate offense to his censorious tone. "I've been as frugal as Ebenezer Scrooge himself, I'm telling you!"

"I'll take a look at your bank and credit statements, but I'm still guessing that you need to live a little less ostentatiously."

Claudette moaned. "Oh, how would that look to the

girls?'' Her hoity-toity social circle spent money as if it were something one harvested in a field.

''Most likely I can cover your debts. This time. But it's time for you to go on a budget.''

''A budget?'' Claudette stared blankly at him.

''Yes. Look it up.'' Sebastian turned and headed for the vast foyer of her country mansion. ''I'll come by later tonight and we'll get started putting one together for you.''

Claudette followed him to the door and watched him slide into his gleaming Peugeot. ''Bring me some of those Bavarian chocolates they serve for dessert.''

Sebastian waved goodbye.

Marie-Claire sensed that Sebastian had arrived even before she saw him. Hearing the slam of a car door had her flying out of the palace's service entrance and straight into his arms. He picked her up and whirled her about and they kissed as if they needed to sustain lip contact to survive.

''You're here!'' Marie-Claire was finally able to say, when they'd paused to gulp in a great lungful of air.

''Mmm.'' Impatiently, Sebastian angled her mouth back under his and went back for seconds. ''Mm-hmm.''

Oh, it was so good to see him. To feel him. To smell him. To taste him. How she'd managed to stay away for so long was a testament to the depth of her heartache over her father's passing. For an endless moment, they stood, basking in the joy of simply being together. Their kiss slowly grew less frenzied and more soulful, and Marie-Claire was lost to this ecstasy. Was there anything more wonderful than falling in love? She didn't think so.

She ran her hands over the powerful planes of Sebastian's chest then locked them at his nape and hung on for dear life as he playfully ravaged her neck. Liquid laughter burbled past her lips. Though she nestled as closely as she could to him, she longed to be even closer, and knew that she'd never truly be happy until she and Sebastian became one forever in the bonds of holy matrimony.

That it would eventually happen, Marie-Claire had no doubt. They were meant to be together. Had been from the very beginning. Their eventual marriage was simply a matter of timing and politics. She closed her eyes and imagined herself in a wedding gown, and that she and Sebastian had just taken their sacred vows to love each other until death parted them. Sebastian's hot mouth on her neck and jaw had her toes curling with delight.

Her sisters could carry on the tedious royal traditions, and she and Sebastian could settle in their own house in his family estate in the country and raise those three little boys and that darling little girl with his striking blue-gray eyes, so eerily translucent and soul-searching. They would also inherit the darling dimples that bracketed the corners of his mouth. Marie-Claire lifted a finger and traced these curves and then ran her fingers down his jaw to the dimple at the apex of his chin. They would have thick, wavy heads of hair, and be filled with life and mischief and they would call her Mama, or Mère…that was cute…*Mère-Claire*…

"Marie-Claire!"

For heaven's sake, why did real life *always* seem to intrude? Frustrated, Marie-Claire's head dropped and she moaned against Sebastian's neck.

"Marie-Claire!" Ariane's voice reached them from the Ruby Salon on the third floor of the de Bergeron Palace. "Sorry to butt in…"

Marie-Claire fumed. "You most certainly are not," she shouted.

Sebastian laughed.

"Yes, I am." Ariane's own laughter blended with Lise's

and floated down to interrupt what had been a dalliance in paradise.

"Then say what you must and go away." Marie-Claire cast them a withering glance.

"Grandmama Simone wants everyone present at lunch for a special announcement. Hi, Sebastian." Again, their girlish giggles.

He waved.

"You are to be included in this meeting, Sebastian."

He groaned.

"What special announcement?" Marie-Claire demanded.

"We don't know. She won't say. But she insists that everyone meet her in the formal dining room in five minutes. She is there waiting now."

The formal dining room?

This was serious. Marie-Claire glanced at Sebastian, her disappointment keen. The Dowager Queen Simone was not one to be ignored, and the formal dining hall always meant a harrowing topic followed by endless and boring discussion.

With great reluctance, Marie-Claire took a step back and, clasping Sebastian's hands in hers, regarded him. "Will this be all right with you? I know you weren't expecting an impromptu meeting on our first day back together."

"It's fine. I'd sit through a presentation on time-share condos if it meant I could be with you."

"Somehow, I doubt it will be anything so painless."

As it was, Sebastian would rather have been gutted, grilled and served for lunch than suffer the tense scene that followed his all-too-brief reunion with Marie-Claire.

They were the first to arrive in the cavernous dining hall and find their pre-assigned seats. Soon after, other family members entered, glanced warily about, took in Queen Simone's dour expression from where she perched on a tall-backed chair at the head of the table, and then cautiously found their own places.

The bowling-lane-sized table was set for the kind of multi-course meal usually reserved for heads of state and very special occasions. A variety of tantalizing aromas wafted through the air ducts from the kitchen—a floor below—as a legion of domestics slaved over the stoves. The de Bergeron insignia blazed from the center of each platter, and the gold charger plates gleamed from a fresh buffing. Myriad pieces of monogrammed silver cluttered each place setting, along with crystal stemware of every size and shape. Sebastian frowned as he pulled his napkin across his lap. Clearly, everyone would need more than one glass of wine to digest the queen's latest bit of news.

The enormous dining hall was as silent as the first day of snow.

No one uttered a word, though it was obvious everyone was wondering about the nature of the dowager queen's command performance. Her stoic expression gave no hint of what was to come, and forbade any queries.

At seventy-five, she was thin as a whip, and it was rumored that she was proud of her skeletal figure and showed it off with expensively tailored garments, nipped in at the waist and snug over the hip. She disdained even a healthy amount of meat on the bones, declaring that it smacked of no self-control. And if there was anything that Simone hated, it was being out of control. Not even the hair on her head dared to defy its perfect coif, dyed dark to belie her age, and snipped short to save time and nonsense. Her eyes were twin chips of ice that rarely sparkled unless it was in irritation.

Lise sat alone, looking decidedly greenish about the gills in these early stages of her pregnancy. Sebastian wondered where Wilhelm was keeping himself, but wasn't surprised at his absence. Trouble had been brewing in paradise since shortly after they'd taken their vows. In a land as small as St. Michel, nothing was sacred, and the private lives and marriages of the royals were frequently discussed over the backyard fence. Or, in Sebastian's mother's case, the cocktail table at the country club where she and "the girls" pretended to play tennis every afternoon.

Ariane sat fidgeting across from her older sister, seemingly eager to dispense with the day's protocol and get on with her own rather guarded agenda.

King Philippe's stepchildren, Georges, twenty-six, and Juliet, twenty-two, and Philippe's fourth daughter, twelve-year-old Jacqueline, by their mother and his second wife, Hélène, all came in together and silently found their seats.

The last to enter was Queen Celeste, her belly burgeoning with the six-month pregnancy that King Philippe had died too soon to celebrate. With a performance worthy of the stage, Celeste, clutching the table attendant's arms, lowered herself into her seat, scooted hither and thither as she fussed with her derriere's perfect arrangement, and then sighed heavily and drummed her fingertips to make everyone aware that she was quite put out at having to sit in such an uncomfortable chair.

After an interminable silence meant to bestow proper ceremony upon the proceedings, Simone at last spoke.

"Thank you all for taking time out of your busy schedule to humor an old lady." A small smile twitched in the corner of her thin lips, and her blue eyes flashed with mystery. "As you all know, many of the legalities concerning my son's death are in the process of being concluded."

Everyone gave a stiff nod, but dared not murmur aloud lest they incur her well-known wrath.

"It is my feeling," she continued, "that sufficient time has passed for grieving. Now, we need to attend to some important issues that should have been addressed years ago. These are personal matters, concerning my son's marriages, and the particulars discussed here will be kept in this room. Is that understood?''

Again, all heads bobbed, and eyes shifted, but no one spoke.

Celeste frowned.

Sebastian fumbled under the tablecloth for Marie-Claire's hand, grasped it and pulled it into his lap. Though her smile was tight, gratitude filled her eyes and she squeezed back. This would be hard on her. She'd only been back for a day and they were about to delve into the private details of Philippe's too-short life.

After giving her throat a lengthy clearing, Queen Simone removed her glasses and seemed to stare off into the distant past.

''As you know, my Philippe was married more than once. But…what you may not know,'' she paused and refocused on Philippe's three oldest daughters, ''is that he was married once before he married your mother, Johanna Van Rhys.''

Ariane and Lise gasped and exchanged shocked glances with Marie-Claire. Sebastian felt Marie-Claire clasp their tightly laced fingers with her free hand as she braced herself for the rest of the story.

''When Philippe was but a boy of eighteen and crown prince, he fell in love with a very beautiful seventeen-year-old American girl named Katie Graham. She had come to St. Michel from her home in Texas with her father, Henry, who was here on business. He'd taken Katie out of school because her mother had recently passed away and he didn't want to leave her alone for the three months it would take him to complete his corporation's business. However, though he'd hoped to keep her from feeling abandoned, it seems he was not entirely successful.

"Henry was occupied most days and had business dinners some nights, so Katie had plenty of time to explore St. Michel all by herself. And one day, while she was out doing so, she met Philippe. It was immediate and deep love from the beginning and no amount of common sense imparted by King Antoine or myself could keep either of them away from the other."

Sebastian glanced at Marie-Claire and knew exactly how Philippe had felt.

"And so," Queen Simone continued, staring now out the window and over the lush, rolling hills beyond the palace walls, "without our knowledge of just how far things had progressed, they ran off to France and were married in a secret, civil ceremony. Needless to say, when Antoine and I found out, we where horrified. Katie's father was a middle-management employee, thus, Katie had no money and no social standing."

Marie-Claire bit her lower lip and, as her eyes slid closed, Sebastian could tell it was all she could do not to scream. Social status meant nothing to Marie-Claire and that was one of the things Sebastian loved best about her. Especially since he'd grown up in a household where aristocracy was everything.

Queen Simone perched her glasses at the tip of her nose, and slowly searched each face with her piercing gaze before she continued. "The magnitude of this misfortune only increased when we learned that the children had married because they were expecting a baby."

The entire room drew in a collective breath and held it.

Marie-Claire's jaw dropped. Ariane grinned in amazement. Looking decidedly ill, Lise covered her face with her hands. Philippe's second wife's children, Georges and Juliet, remained silent, as Philippe was not their real father, and this news did not particularly affect them. And Philippe's youngest girl, Jacqueline, was but twelve and the ramifications were over her head.

Celeste seemed to have forgotten her discomfort and stared at Simone with rapt attention. Jaw jutting, eyes glittering, she cradled her own unborn babe with protective arms.

Queen Simone fiddled with the soft fringe at the edge of her shawl and sighed noisily through her nose as the memories came flooding back. "Because St. Michel had been threatened with annexation by Rhineland we needed some clout and had hoped that Philippe would make a politically advantageous marriage. In fact, our very freedom depended on it. We had no choice, Antoine and I. We did what we thought best."

By this time, everyone was hanging on her every word. All eyes watched as the dowager queen pressed her thumbnails together, and searched for the proper words to best explain her actions of over thirty years ago.

"We...Philippe's father, Antoine, and I...we decided that it would be in the best interest of the children to tell them that..." Queen Simone's words grew halting with long-forgotten emotion. Hands shaking, she pressed the fringe of her shawl to her quivering lips and waited until she felt able to continue.

The tension in the room was so high, Sebastian believed it could power the chandelier. The wine stewards must have sensed this too and moved in with loaded magnums to fill the wine goblets.

Forcing herself to stay on track, no matter how painful, Queen Simone continued.

"Antoine and I told the children that their marriage was not legal because Katie was underage, and had not received her father's permission. Katie's father, Henry, did not know enough about French law to dispute our claim, and neither did the kids. We were afraid that if they tried to get an annulment, since they would both be required to sign, that one or both of them might refuse, so we did not press for that.

"Further, this would have revealed that the marriage *was* legal and would have given both Katie and her father the opportunity to take advantage of the situation. Then heaven only knows what would have happened. My husband, King Antoine, told Henry that if he told anyone about this scandalous affair that we would pressure his corporation—where poor Henry had been working for twenty years—to fire him. We knew that his company had a huge vested interest in doing business with St. Michel and other European countries related to St. Michel and that we had Henry over the proverbial barrel."

Simone leaned back in her chair, seeming to shrink and age considerably as she did so. Outside, a cloud eclipsed the sun and the room darkened perceptibly.

"So, we gave Henry a substantial amount of money to remain silent. Henry, who was very conservative, was not anxious to broadcast his daughter's 'shame' anyway, so he took the deal and the money. As far as we know, they went back to Texas. We have never heard from them again."

Simone tented her gnarled fingers before her lips for a moment, pondering what she would say next.

Marie-Claire glanced up at Sebastian, her cheeks pale, and eyes bright with myriad emotions that would no doubt be surfacing for days to come. He gave her hand a little squeeze and she leaned into him, drawing strength and comfort from their touch, much the way she had in the days after her father had passed away.

"All right." Queen Simone pushed herself up in her seat and hauled her rounded shoulders back into bony points. "The down side of all this—"

Marie-Claire stared up at Sebastian and mouthed the words *"down side?"* Apprehension filled her eyes, and Sebastian adjusted his position so that their arms and thighs touched, hoping the contact would calm her.

"—is that we were never sure that the marriage had been annulled. If, as we suspect, Katie and Philippe's marriage was never absolved, then Philippe's marriage to the Dutch princess Johanna Van Rhys was invalid, as well as his subsequent marriages."

She let that sink in a moment before announcing, "Which, of course, would make Phillipe's four daughters and unborn child illegitimate. The icing on this rather botched cake would be that we never did learn the sex of Katie's baby. If this baby was a boy...and if he is still alive...he would now be St. Michel's crown prince."

Chapter Four

"The reason I even bring this up now," Queen Simone explained to her dumbstruck family, "is that St. Michel's government is a monarchy based on primogeniture, which, as you all know, means that the throne passes through the male line. If there is no male heir to the throne, there is a very real threat that St. Michel will be...will be..." she faltered, swallowed and began again, "...will be absorbed by our neighbors in Rhineland, of which it was part until the seventeenth century."

Expression pensive, Simone hunched forward.

"In Rhineland, there is a faction that has been plotting to take over St. Michel. It's all economics. As you are all aware, we have the St. Michel River inside our border by a good kilometer. It's the only way to the North Sea from here. And...from Rhineland. They've grown weary of paying us for its usage. With the king's death, they have begun to make serious plans to gain control not only of the river, but of our government as well."

Slowly, Simone rubbed her gnarled knuckles with her thumbs.

"These people present a grave threat to the freedoms we enjoy as a small nation. So far, they have only issued idle threats, but make no mistake. These people are dangerous. There is little conscience to stop them from taking what they want, and so it is up to us to create a united, organized front, with an heir firmly in place before this goes any further."

Celeste stopped drumming her fingertips. No one moved. Silence fell like a coastal fog before dawn.

Horrified, Marie-Claire glanced up at Sebastian and could see the truth of her grandmother's words reflected in his eyes. She felt numb from head to foot. How could she, just six short months ago, have been leading such a carefree life? Before Papa died, her only concerns were catching Sebastian's eye and shopping in Paris.

Now, her whole world seemed to be shifting on its axis. The security of her homeland was being threatened, she had an older sibling she'd never met, and to top it all off, she was most likely illegitimate.

The sun was still hidden and now, ominous thunderclouds were rolling in, echoing the dark nature of what was happening here at the table today. Marie-Claire squirmed in her seat, feeling suddenly claustrophobic and desperate to get away. To run somewhere, anywhere with Sebastian and to cry and rage against life's little injustices.

And those not so little.

"We know," Queen Simone's wavering falsetto again captured all eyes, "that this faction in Rhineland has heard the news of our missing heir, but are not yet worried about this, assuming that either the heir will not be found, or she will be a girl, given Philippe's history."

Celeste could not stand being ignored another moment.

With a sudden explosion of fury, she battled her way out of her chair. Arms akimbo, face flaming, veins popping, she barreled, belly-first, toward the dowager queen.

"*My baby* is next in line for the throne! *My baby* is a *male!* My baby is legitimate! How *dare* you all discount *my baby,* who is Philippe's last gift to us all, and go off searching for some *fairytale heir* who was most likely *never even born!*"

Ever unflappable, Simone dismissed Celeste's outrage. "You won't have so much as an ultrasound, so how can we know if you are having a boy? This is your first baby. You have a fifty-fifty chance. I won't bet this kingdom on those dismal odds. Besides, how can we be sure that the baby you are carrying is even Philippe's? Philippe has been gone for as many months as you are pregnant. I find this last-second production of an heir suspiciously convenient."

Shaking like the tail of a coiled rattler, Celeste gripped the back of an empty chair as murder glittered in her eyes. "You will regret that insinuation, old lady."

"Perhaps you should go lie down, Celeste," Simone suggested placidly. "You're not looking so well."

Celeste hovered for a moment then thrust away the chair she clutched. A cold smile crept across her lips, but not into her eyes. "For the sake of the *true heir* to St. Michel's throne, I will rest now."

And with that, she turned and swept out of the room.

Queen Simone signaled for the dining-room attendants to begin serving the first course. While they bustled about, she lifted her goblet and everyone joined her in tossing back a deep drink of wine.

As she prepared to make her next announcement, she blotted her thin lips on a fine linen napkin and swallowed a delicate burp.

"I feel it is time for us to bring in an investigator from

the St. Michel Security Force, and the prime minister has recently secured a good man by the name of Luc Dumont to find Philippe and Katie's child and to determine if this child is indeed a male.'' She let this news digest a bit then asked, ''Any questions?''

Still shell-shocked from the bomb she'd just dropped, everyone simply stared, unseeing, deep in thought about how all this news would affect each of their lives.

Though the clouds that hovered over the western horizon were black and heavy with unshed rain, the air was unusually humid. The minute Marie-Claire and Sebastian stepped outside the palace and left the comfort of the climate-controlled rooms, Marie-Claire began to wilt. Thank God for Sebastian's strong arm. And, though the two glasses of wine on her still-empty stomach were somewhat fortifying, she was devastated all over again. She thought she'd spent the previous six months crying out the last of her tears, but here they were, hovering at the edge of her lower lashes again.

Sebastian pulled her hand to his lips and kissed her palm as they walked, and, unable to speak for fear she'd start crying and be powerless to stop, she swallowed and blinked and kept pace with him.

Together they strolled through the blossoming gardens in a comfortable silence. And though they had no particular destination in mind, they moved with purpose, past *Le cheval du roi* fountain, through the fabulous glass-walled greenhouses, around various gazebos and on down the gravel path that led beyond the rolling lawn toward the small valley that sheltered the stables from bad weather.

Sebastian moved with an easy masculinity that still thoroughly captivated Marie-Claire. He always seemed so calm. So sure of himself. Able to ride out even the wildest storm without a trace of damage. She glanced down at her hand, enveloped in his stronger, larger one and was bolstered at the sight.

The shadows were lengthening across the lawn and birds twittered from the acres of forest that edged the numerous manicured garden areas. Off on a neighboring farm, cattle lowed as they headed inside for their evening milking.

Just strolling along together was incredibly calming, and Marie-Claire realized that, for the first time in a long while, she felt safe. It was almost as if, with Sebastian by her side, she could face any obstacle life might toss her way. The knots in her stomach loosened some, and the burning lump in her throat began to subside. As if he understood, Sebastian kissed her temple and Marie-Claire was consumed with love for him.

The stables that loomed just ahead had been her favorite place of escape as a child. To her, they meant freedom. She'd learned to ride at an early age and before entering her teens had won a number of prestigious equestrian competitions. She felt as at home on the back of a horse as she did in a rocking chair and so it was natural that she'd unconsciously steer Sebastian to this destination, when she was hurting.

Together they entered the now-silent main stable. Though daylight poured through the doors and windows, the lights were burning in the broad hallway. Out in the paddock, trainers worked a number of horses, leaving Marie-Claire and Sebastian alone for the time being.

The pungent aroma of horse sweat, fresh manure and sweet hay, mingled with the musty scent of old wood and slowly drifting dust motes. Eyes closed, Marie-Claire filled her lungs and believed she could smell the medieval history radiating from the ancient walls and floor.

She paused, with Sebastian at her side, and listened intently, straining to hear the past, both distant and recent. The stomping hooves and impatient snorts echoed those from centuries gone by. The faint reverberation in the back of her mind came from a time when St. Michel had had to fight for its precious freedoms.

And the stronger sounds were born of times of peace— her papa's low laughter, a horse's eager whinny and the wind whistling as they flew.

Marie-Claire drew Sebastian past a dozen stalls till she reached her father's horse, Sovereign's Golden Boy. Low nickers rumbled forth as his thoroughbred head protruded from the stall to greet his visitors. Ears twitching, he watched their approach with soulful brown eyes. His nostrils flared and blew as he strained to reach them.

Marie-Claire buried her nose in the horse's neck and inhaled the serenity she always found here. "Hey, handsome. How about a kiss for your girl?"

Golden Boy lipped her cheek and snorted through her hair and after a bit of a slobber that could be construed by a creative mind as a kiss, he pulled back his whiskered lips and seemed to send Sebastian a challenging grin.

"Should I be jealous?" Sebastian wondered.

"Mm-hmm." With a coy smile, she nodded and reached for a carrot in the pail behind her. "He's mine now," she murmured. "Lise, Juliet and Ariane weren't interested, Jacqueline was too young and Papa knew I had loved him since he was a foal."

"Beautiful."

He was stroking the horse, but she knew his eyes were on her as she let Golden Boy lip the carrot from her palm. An exhilarating flutter of physical awareness bubbled in her belly. Unsettled by his blatant interest, she strove to appear as if the look in his dark, bedroom eyes had no effect on the strength of her knees or the steadiness of her hands. She touched her tongue to her suddenly dry lips and searched for a change of subject.

"I'm so sorry you were subjected to that..." Marie-Claire groped for the words as she pushed away from Golden Boy's neck and went to the tack room for a set of curry-combs, "that...scene at dinner." She was glad he couldn't see the flames of embarrassment that licked her cheeks. "Had I known that Grandmama was going to sort the dirty laundry at the dining-room table, I'd never have invited you for tonight."

"Marie-Claire, your papa was like a father to me, too. He always had a way of making me feel a part of his life. Of his family. And all families have their good conversations and their bad conversations."

"Yes, but seldom do the skeletons come flying out of the closet at such a rate without benefit of air-traffic control." When she emerged from the tack room she handed a brush to Sebastian and kept one for herself.

Sebastian chuckled. "I have to admit I learned a few things about your family tonight." Together, they tethered her horse just outside his stall and set to work brushing his satin coat to a high sheen.

"So did I." Her mouth curved in a rueful twist as she laid her cheek upon Golden Boy's smooth flank. "I wonder why Papa never mentioned Katie to any of us?"

Sebastian paused in his grooming of the horse's broad chest and shrugged. "It was a long time ago. He probably didn't think it was relevant any longer."

"Not relevant? Sebastian, they had a baby together! I'd say that might be worth mentioning."

Snuffing and blowing, Golden Boy swung his head down, and lipped Sebastian's hair. Good-naturedly, Sebastian patted his nose, then nudged him away and continued brushing.

"As king, your father was in a precarious position. Sometimes the hint of scandal in the tabloids can bring a country as small as ours to its knees.''

"Yes, but we're his *family*. I'd have liked to have known I had another sibling before now. After all, this person would have to be..." she did some mental calculating and stared at Sebastian, "...as old as you!" Her jaw sagged. "That's ancient."

"Sebastian, I'm trying to be serious here." She squinted at him. "You don't have any old wives and children that may come popping out of the woodwork any time soon, do you?"

Sebastian took a step and gathered her in his arms and rocked her playfully. "No wives and definitely no children. Although, I might be persuaded to get to working on that, if you were in the mood." He nuzzled her neck, sending great waves of gooseflesh sailing down her back and arms.

Marie-Claire reared back and, unable to help herself, laughed. "You are terrible." She stared into his mesmerizing blue eyes for a long time, and felt herself go limp. "I feel so sorry for Papa," she whispered.

"Why?"

"To have this...and then to lose it."

"We won't let that happen."

"Promise?"

"Mmm." He pulled her close and gently kissed her lips. "I promise."

"I don't understand how he could have married my mother, not knowing what had become of his first love and his baby."

"It was a more complicated time, back then. He had to fulfill his duty and bring an heir to the throne."

"We'll never know, now that they are both dead, but I wonder if that's why he really divorced my mother," Marie-Claire mused. Hands dangling behind his neck, she plucked at the coarse bristles of the currycomb she still held. "Siring three daughters was not the most auspicious start on his legacy."

"No, but I know he loved you without reserve."

Marie-Claire felt her throat grow tight. "I know. But I don't think he ever really loved Mum. She was too wild."

"Like you?"

A tiny smile teased Marie-Claire's lips. "More so. She wanted to be a freedom fighter. And a firefighter. And a bullfighter. She was an awesome woman. But she never should have been a mother. She died in a scuba-diving accident, somewhere near the Great Barrier Reef on one of her endless—and infamous—vacations."

"Philippe never mentioned that."

"Guilt, I'd imagine. Their divorce was a bit acrimonious."

"Still, you're spontaneous, like her."

Marie-Claire lifted a shoulder and cast him a lopsided grin. "Unfortunately true." Slowly, her hands traveled from his broad shoulders and over his powerful chest. Not trusting the sudden impulses she felt to unbutton his placket and to see if his chest was really as smooth and hard as she'd dreamed, she turned and began to vigorously brush Golden Boy's mane.

Sebastian set back to work himself. "Marriages of convenience are not unheard of even in this day and age," he mused. "Chances are he needed her for their positive political alliance, but probably wasn't in love with her."

"Or Hélène, for that matter."

He glanced over his shoulder. "I think there was probably some sympathy happening there, being that Hélène was his old friend's widow. But again, a political alliance was advantageous for everyone."

"That's just so...*sad.*" She wrapped several coarse

strands of Golden Boy's mane around her forefinger and, try as she might, could remember neither her father's divorce from her mother, nor his marriage to Hélène when she was only three. "I'm sure that had a lot to do with it. Papa felt sorry for Hélène and her children, Georges and Juliet." She finger-combed the horse's forelock and kissed his soft, whiskery nose. "Poor Hélène. She was so desperate to prove herself worthy by bearing Papa a son."

"That's how she died, isn't it?"

"Mm-hmm. The first baby boy was stillborn and that shattered her. When Jacqueline came along she fell into a terrible depression, and by the time she gave birth to her last baby, she simply did not have the strength. She and the boy both died within hours of one another. I'm not sure she ever even knew it was a boy."

A low sound of sympathy rumbled from Sebastian and he glanced at her with a look that spoke of his unconditional love. Of a love that transcended their stations in life and their age difference. A love that Marie-Claire knew would see them through battles both personal and political. A love that would overlook bad hair and cramps and graying heads and wrinkles.

Sweet and at the same time wildly exciting, it was the love Marie-Claire had craved her entire life. The kind of love her father had enjoyed for but a fleeting moment in his youth.

"Papa carried a lot of guilt for Hélène's death. That guilt and a healthy dose of mid-life crisis led him to Celeste, I think." Marie-Claire's laugh was mirthless. "I cannot imagine what else would have blinded him to her...her," she grimaced, "...imperfections."

"A beautiful face will lure a man into all kinds of trouble." He winked at Marie-Claire, and she responded with a cheeky smile.

Sebastian moved into the tack room and Marie-Claire could hear him rummaging. He returned with a saddle blanket, a saddle and a bridle. These he dropped on the ground, save for the blanket, which he tossed up over the horse's back.

"Still," Marie-Claire began, too lost in thought to really ponder his actions, then dropped to a bale of hay and tucked a straw into the corner of her mouth, "it's all very tragic. I'd be willing to bet that Papa never found true love again after Katie. I wonder whatever happened to her. To her baby."

Sebastian hefted the saddle up over the horse's back and reached under his belly for the girth. He was as comfortable in the barn as he was in the boardroom, she noted idly. She watched as, with deft fingers, he adjusted the stirrups. Oh, but he was handsome. And all male. Beneath his snug polo shirt, rugged muscles flexed and her eyes followed his smooth motions. He would age nicely, she decided, taking in the distinguished silver threads at his temples and the tiny lines at the corners of his eyes.

Just like her papa.

Sebastian and her father had a lot in common. A zest for life. A gentle, yet decisive nature. Above average height. King Philippe would have loved to have had him as a son-in-law, she just knew.

The sobering memories of her father had sudden tears stinging the backs of her eyes and a burning lump of emotion lodging in her throat.

Sebastian swung into the saddle and, as if he could read the direction of her thoughts, extended his hand.

"Come on," he instructed. She didn't hesitate and, in an inkling, she was seated in front of him. "Let's get away for awhile."

In his sparse apartment in St. Michel's capital city, St. Michel, Luc Dumont hung up the phone and sank to the edge of his lumpy bed. He'd just been on the line with the offices at Interpol, the international police force, and a few pieces of his latest puzzle were beginning to fall into place.

He scanned the fax they'd just sent of the thirty-three-year-old marriage certificate and the faded blurb in a small French newspaper announcing the marriage of Philippe de Bergeron and Katie Graham.

Luc frowned. Either Philippe had bought the silence of the county clerks, or they'd worn some sort of disguise, because the news of St. Michel's crown prince's marriage should have been the stuff of a front-page headline, not a brief mention buried in the milestones column.

> Katie Graham, 17, student, Houston, Texas, U.S.A.,
> and Philippe de Bergeron, 18, student, St. Michel,
> were wed in a civil ceremony,
> Tuesday, July 22, 1969.

There were no pictures, but Luc imagined that, as teenagers, they were baby-faced innocents. He stared, unseeing, at a crude watercolor of the Eiffel Tower that clung to his wall and wondered at the fate of this woman and her baby.

In a way, he could commiserate with this mystery child. He knew what it was like to lose a parent at an early age. This royal baby had never known his father. Luc, on the other hand, had lost his mother when he was only six.

He shook his head. Raw deal, but those were the breaks.

He reached for the phone and considered calling his father and telling him that he was working a big, prestigious case, knowing that Albert would be proud. It would be early morning, stateside. Albert's wife, Jeanne, would still be home. On second thought, Luc set the handset back in its cradle. Jeanne had never liked Luc. He'd always figured it was because he resembled his mother. Riddled with insecurities, Jeanne was the reason he'd grown up in boarding schools. Even now, he avoided contact with her whenever he could.

He'd call later, he decided. After Jeanne went to bed.

Sovereign's Golden Boy was surefooted and his canter smooth as Sebastian and Marie-Claire rode down the gravel road, away from the stables. Off in the distance, the setting sun peeked through a clear spot in the black thunderheads, causing a perfect—nearly neon in its intensity—rainbow to curve over the deep forest that loomed ahead. Wind whipped through Marie-Claire's hair, twining strands around Sebastian's neck as he held her firmly against his body.

Instinctively, Sebastian led them to the edge of the trees, and slowed, picking his way toward their pond. Marie-Claire twisted around and looked up at him with a smile that he was sure only he could understand.

After wending their way through the underbrush, they emerged at the outcropping of rock that protruded over the water's edge. Over the years, not a thing had changed. Even the weather was the same. Humid. Sultry. Charged with electricity. A rumble of thunder clapped beyond the hills and overhead, fat, warm drops spattered to earth. One at a time. For now.

The deluge was to come, Sebastian was sure. Of both rain and emotion.

Without words, Sebastian handed Marie-Claire to the ground. After he'd spent some time tethering Golden Boy, he turned and looked up to find her poised at the edge of the rock. His jaw worked and his mouth went dry at the sight. She'd removed her sandals and sweater, but still wore the filmy white sundress she'd worn to lunch. Seemingly the heavens had sent down an angel as the twilight sun set her hair aflame with a golden haze. The dark shadows of her long, shapely legs were backlit beneath her translucent skirt.

Sebastian felt as if he'd stepped back in time, only now, Marie-Claire was a full-fledged woman. Fire kindled in his belly and he stood watching her, unable to move. Her slow gaze traveled to his and locked. In silent communion, they stood, intrinsically knowing things about each other that no one else ever could.

He studied the emotions that flitted across her face.

He could feel the depth of her sorrow. Her feelings of betrayal, inspired by Simone's shocking news. And, the fierce devotion she held for him. These emotions seemed to war within until she was driven to escape.

Taking flight, she executed a graceful arc and dove into the pool below. This time, she surfaced immediately, shook her head and the poignant look on her face spoke of a loss of innocence. His throat tight, Sebastian mourned for that carefree girl, even as he fell in love with this evolving woman.

As she waded toward him, water ran in rivulets from her hair, over her face, landing in sparkling droplets on her full lips. Her thin sheath clung to her body, drawing him inexorably toward her.

Stripping off his shirt, he waded waist-deep into the water and pulled her into his arms. With the pads of his thumbs, he smoothed the drops—tears or water, he couldn't be sure—from her cheeks and lips.

"Don't worry," he whispered. His chin grazed hers as he spoke.

Gaze plaintive, she stared up at him, her arms locked at his waist. "I don't even know who I am anymore."

"I do."

"Who then?"

"The other half of me."

Her eyes fell shut and her sigh was sweet against his cheeks.

"It will all work out." He only wished he was as assured as he sounded. Feeling suddenly afraid that his words rang false, he pulled her close and kissed her with a fierce possession that rivaled any emotion he'd ever experienced before.

Though Marie-Claire was famished and chilled as they rode back to the stables on Golden Boy, the strong arms that kept her firmly in place in the saddle fortified her. Sebastian's chest was warm and solid against her back, and Marie-Claire nestled against him, cupping his biceps with her palms. The five o'clock stubble that shadowed his jaw caught strands of her hair, giving her an excuse to occasionally reach up and brush his lips with the hills of her knuckles.

He smiled down at her with a look that couldn't have felt any more intimate than if they'd made love, back there on the sweet spring grass. But they hadn't.

It would have been wrong.

As excited as they'd been, they both heard the powerful echo of her father's voice cautioning them to live up to the royal code of ethics and morals. To make him proud, even now, in his absence.

And since Sebastian was an honorable man, he'd mustered his last shred of willpower to tear his lips from hers and set her away from him. Even though his labored breathing told her that he'd been just as tortured to stop at kisses as she was.

Marie-Claire heaved a disgruntled sigh. She'd never listened to Papa when he was alive. Why start now? She peeked up at Sebastian's rugged jaw, hovering just over her shoulder and knew the truth.

Because this was more than merely important. Sebastian was her soul mate. The first time they came together, it had to be perfect. And right.

Soon, she promised herself. Soon enough, they would be man and wife. And they would spend whole days in bed together. Marie-Claire shivered at the vivid thoughts that exploded in her mind and—thinking she was cold—Sebastian held her tighter and kissed her neck, which only caused her to shiver again.

"We'll be home soon," he murmured.

"Mmm." Not nearly soon enough.

When they'd put Golden Boy up for the night, they rushed to the palace and sneaked in through the servants' entrance and into the kitchen. While they raided the pantry for leftovers, wearing terrycloth robes, one of the evening housekeepers dried their clothes. They made banal conversation, designed to convince the staff that there was nothing going on between them.

As they ate, Marie-Claire had to wonder at the success of their ruse. She could see the knowing glances and small smiles exchanged by the kitchen staff in the reflection of several large windows. No doubt rumors would be flying by morning. She didn't care. Sooner or later, the world would figure out that little Marie-Claire de Bergeron was all grown up and madly in love.

"I wish you didn't have to go," she murmured a short time later as they stood in the shadows just outside the servants' entrance.

"Me, too, but we've given them enough to wonder about for one night, don't you think?"

"You noticed the cooks whispering while we ate?"

Marie-Claire swallowed against the mirth that rose into her throat.

"No. But I think several of them are watching us now. Either that, or they enjoy standing at the window with their faces smashed to the glass."

"Where?" Laughter spurted past her lips.

"Shhh. Don't look, or they'll know we can see them."

"What should we do?"

"Depends."

"On what?"

"On what you want them to think."

"What are my options?"

"Well…" He rubbed his jaw and looked up into the night sky. "We could shake hands and I could pound you on the back, like a buddy."

Marie-Claire thrust out her lower lip. "That's no fun."

"Or, I could make an inappropriate advance, and you could slap me…"

"Definitely more interesting, but I'm a lover, not a slapper."

Sebastian groaned. He took a deep breath. "Okay, we could walk over to my car, where they can't see us, and I could give you a proper kiss goodnight. Let them wonder."

Marie-Claire's eyes dropped to half-mast as a tempest of elation rose and fell in her belly. "I choose that last one."

"Me, too. C'mon."

Every second that Sebastian lingered in the shadows with Marie-Claire, it became harder to leave. It was only the knowledge that the watchful eye of the security cameras could capture images that would make their private life a public circus, that enabled him to leave.

At times like this, he hated the fact that she was of royal blood and wished that instead she was the peasant girl he'd originally taken her for when she was sixteen. Then nobody would care about the stupid details of her life. She'd be able to be with whomever she pleased without having to pause and think about how her actions would affect a nation.

As he lifted his hand in a parting wave and pulled his car onto the circular drive, he rotated his head to dispel the tension. He considered turning around and coaxing her to disappear with him. They'd elope. Leave St. Michel forever and live life on their own terms. Surely, they'd be happier as paupers not having to deal with the idiotic protocol that went with living as a royal.

Sebastian could empathize with Philippe and Katie. The thought of bucking the system and living life on his own terms was powerfully seductive. Although not realistic. Their life was here. In St. Michel. Soon enough, they would be married. Living as one. Forever.

Overhead, a bolt of lightening split the sky and Sebastian had to turn on his windshield wipers as rain began to fall in buckets. The weather was the perfect complement to his foul mood. He squinted at the road, his mouth twisting sourly.

For propriety's sake, they would have to be engaged for at least six months before they could be married. And the time of mourning for King Philippe would be over as well. Until then, he'd have to endure being stalked by various and sundry security guards and chaperones and live for stolen moments.

Just ahead, the road forked, one way leading to his house, the other to his mother's. Sebastian passed a hand over his face and heaving a tired sigh, turned down the road that lead to Claudette's. He knew his mother would be anxiously awaiting details of his lunch at the castle, eager for juicy tidbits of royal gossip.

Lights blazed in every room of his mother's house and as Sebastian parked his car, he made a mental note to lecture her on the finer points of conservation.

Brandy swirled into matching snifters as Claudette poured from her private reserve. While she busied herself, Sebastian relaxed by the fire that roared in her magnificent hearth and allowed his gaze to travel over the eclectic décor his mother had foisted upon the once-clean lines of this elegant room. Clutter from every corner of the earth abounded, making the walls close in, leaving little open space. Expensive shelving units had been erected to hold all nature of bric-a-brac and collectibles meant to impress visitors with her taste and wealth. No inch went undecorated; the walls were covered with art, the tables with treasures and the floor with furniture and rugs.

Sebastian's gaze drifted about, noting new additions to the chaos, and he sighed. The likelihood that Claudette would learn to control her impulse spending seemed nil. No doubt she would land in bankruptcy court before she would part with a single treasure. The prospect of an evening spent sorting her scrambled records had his head suddenly throbbing.

Outside, the wind screamed over the countryside and rain poured in sheets down her windows. Inside, his eyes slid closed and he fell into a dreamy twilight filled with blissful thoughts of Marie-Claire until his mother's shrill voice startled him to wakefulness.

"Well? Are you going to just sit there, or are you going to tell me what went on up at the palace today?"

Sebastian sighed and took the glass that she'd thrust under his nose. "Of course. What do you want to know?"

"Everything!" She squinted at him. "But first, tell me why, now that Philippe is dead, were you invited to dine with the family? It's not as if you are intimate with any of them.''

"True enough.'' Amused, Sebastian felt a wry grin tug at his lips. Not just yet, anyway. Since his budding relationship with Marie-Claire was still far too private to share with anyone, let alone his meddlesome mother, he decided to steer her toward information he knew would become public knowledge within the next few weeks. "Perhaps they invited me because they know of my business ties with Rhineland.''

Claudette stared at her son, expression baffled. "What has Rhineland to do with anything?''

"You will hear this soon enough, I suppose.'' Sebastian took a thoughtful sip of brandy. "Since Philippe's death, there is a faction in Rhineland that is plotting to reabsorb St. Michel into their government. Simone wanted to ask me what I knew about the political climate over there and some of the nuances of negotiation with their government officials.''

Claudette huffed over the rim of her glass as she rested it against her ruby lips. Clearly this was not the kind of personal buzz she was looking for. "Why would we worry about Rhineland? We seceded centuries ago. Why the sudden fuss?''

"Because now there is no heir to the throne. And—'' though he knew he probably shouldn't confide anything more intimate than the weather report with Claudette, he continued in hopes of dousing the flames of curiosity with a thimbleful of information, "apparently Philippe may have another child. My age. Perhaps a boy. If they can find him, he would be crown prince.''

Lips pursed, Claudette's gaze darted to his and she swallowed. Hard. After a long, frozen moment she queried, "What?''

"Remember, St. Michel is a monarchy that passes through the male line." Sebastian leaned back in his chair and crossed his legs on top of the leather ottoman. "Aside from Celeste's baby, our only hope of remaining independent is finding this possible first-born son to ascend to the throne. It seems there is some question as to whether Celeste's baby is even Philippe's, let alone a male, which makes locating this missing heir even more important."

Claudette froze, eyes glazed, the wheels in her brain processing this new information. Finally, she touched her tongue to her suddenly parched lips and managed to croak. "Missing heir?"

"They've hired the head of St. Michel's security force to find him."

She stared at Sebastian, but her eyes saw only the images that whirled in her mind. Her breathing had become shallow, and her glass tilted, a bit of brandy spilled upon her lap. She did not notice. "This heir. You say...he would be the crown prince," she murmured.

"Mm. About my age."

"Yes. Exactly your age."

"Seems Philippe was married to an American teenager named—" Sebastian frowned, struggling to recall her name.

"Katie."

"Yes! That's—" Brow arched, he glanced at his mother. "How did you know about Katie?"

Claudette opened her mouth to speak, but could only emit tiny, guttural sounds, as if she were choking. Sebastian pulled his legs off the ottoman and leaning toward her took the glass from her hands and set it on a nearby table. Concerned, he watched the blood rush into her neck and cheeks. Tiny beads of sweat formed on her upper lip and she trembled.

"Mère, what is it?"

Hands to her cheeks, Claudette gawped at him, her mouth working, struggling to form the necessary words. ''I never wanted to tell you.'' Her eyes brimmed with tears.

Outside, thunder roared and seconds later a flash of lightning lit the room. The power failed and a sudden feeling of doom clutched at Sebastian's heart as the firelight flickered over his mother's tortured expression, and he forced himself to ask what he was quite sure he wouldn't want to know.

''Tell me what?''

Chapter Five

Claudette clutched Sebastian's hands till he was certain she'd drawn blood. Like a carp plucked from the lake and gasping for precious oxygen, she gurgled. He'd never known her to be so afraid of the dark.

"Mère?" Sebastian prompted. Claudette had always possessed a flair for the dramatic but even so, her rigid countenance and glassy-eyed stare was unusual. Unnerving.

Outside, the storm raged. Inside, Sebastian could feel one brewing. He disentangled his hand from Claudette's clutches long enough to fumble through an end table's clutter for some candles and matches. Once he'd lit these, his mother's face was less shadowed but no less contorted.

Wind screamed through the ancient window casings and thunder, like the rumble of an earthquake, vibrated overhead, rattling the decorative plates perched upon the mantle. Immediately following, a flash of lightning rent the gloaming, and, as Sebastian glanced out the window, he felt an uncommon chill snake down his spine. Against the blinding light, the trees stood stark, crooked branches beckoning like the bony fingers of the grim reaper.

Sebastian raked a hand over his jaw and snorted.

He was letting his mother's imagination run away with him. Even Claudette's master manipulation couldn't produce the squall outside and its colliding weather fronts. The electricity in the air was simply that, and had no deeper, evil nuances.

Whatever she was about to tell him was no doubt simply a tempest on the tennis court. Some local gossip that would have nothing to do with him. As soon as the lights came back on, he'd persuade her to gather her financial papers and a calculator and they'd begin wading through the mess that was Claudette's filing system.

He found their brandy glasses, topped them off and handed one to his mother. "Mère, try to relax. It's just a storm. The lights will be back on soon."

Claudette moaned and dropped her chin to her bosom. "If only it were that easy."

Sebastian rotated his head to ease the tension. And irritation. "What? If only what were that easy?"

Claudette's flighty gaze glanced to his face. Remembering the brandy she held, she tossed back a slug, wincing and shuddering as it blazed its way down her throat. Through her nostrils, she sucked in a deep breath and then dabbed her mouth on the back of her wrist. "I've kept this from you, because I felt it was for your own good."

Okay. Here it came. She'd bought ocean-front property in Antarctica or some other such lunacy. Impatient with her, Sebastian dropped into the club chair by the fire and crossed his feet atop the ottoman. Leaning back, he let his eyes slide to half mast, and exhaled his long day into the shadows. This was going to take a while.

"Go on."

Trembling, Claudette pressed her lacquered fingertips to her lips and spoke in muffled phrases. "I had to do it. Because I was protecting her. And him. Everyone."

"Her? Him? Who?"

"I was there. At the wedding. It's all true."

"What wedding? What's true?" He squeezed his eyes shut as a nebulous foreboding filled his belly. What was she up to now?

"She was pregnant. Her father was so angry. He was working class. A nobody. The boy's father and mother were horrified. There was nothing anyone could do. So they decided to have the baby quietly, and then give him up, to…to…to…"

"Mère, could you go back to the beginning and clue me in as to who the devil you're talking about?"

"…to…to a childless couple. A couple she believed could not have children of their own, though they were desperate for a baby…"

Another unnerving clap of thunder forced her to momentary silence. When she resumed speaking, the corresponding bolt of light that filled the room amplified her dry, raspy words and bleached her turbulent expression.

"That couple…was us."

"What the devil are you talking about?"

"You."

Sebastian moved not a muscle.

"*You!*" Claudette shrieked then began to blubber into her bejeweled hands. "You are that child."

Tiny hairs on the back of Sebastian's neck stood at attention and as he stared at his mother, realization slowly dawned. He stared at her for a long, electric minute, his mind attempting to make sense of her jumbled information. He filled his lungs and deliberately kept his voice low.

"Are you trying to tell me that I am not your son?"

They stared at each other until Claudette could take the strain no longer and, with a tortured moan, propped her elbows on the arm of her chair and buried her face in the great folds of her sleeves.

"You will always be my son! It's just…it's just that you…Katie…Philippe…I always wanted a baby, and she…well, she had no recourse. She was an American. So young. There was so much at stake. The reputation of the crown prince, the future of the monarchy…*Ohh*."

Claudette's ghoulish wails rivaled the wind that shrieked through the valley. She snatched a handful of tissues from a silver dispenser at her elbow and alternately blew and mopped.

"Mère, if you think this is funny, you are wrong."

"Sebastian, my darling, I have never…" her mouth worked, her eyes glazed, "I have never been more… more…*serious* about anything. I…I have proof. Documentation. With a few phone calls I'm reasonably sure I can get it for you in the morning."

The muscles in his jaw jerked and his eyes narrowed. "Why have you waited until now to tell me?"

Her lips were now a smeared slash of ruby red and fiery spots of guilt over this late-in-the-day admission stained her cheeks. Brackish rivers ran from her eyes, over her mouth and drip, drip, dripped onto her hands.

"I never *wanted* to tell you. Your father and I loved you as if you were our own flesh and blood. There was nothing more sacred to us than your happiness. We knew that growing up with the stigma of having been rejected by the royals would have been a horrible cross to bear for a little child."

Sebastian jumped to his feet, took several steps back and could only stare at this woman he thought he'd known all his life. It was almost as if she were speaking a different language, so foreign were her words.

"And it didn't seem to matter that you were of royal blood. After all, Philippe has many children that could ascend to the throne."

"All female."

"Yes. Girls." Claudette lifted hands of supplication, imploring him to understand. "But until you just reminded me, I'd quite forgotten that St. Michel required a *male* heir. It's been so long since we've needed a crown prince, and King Philippe and Celeste seemed to have a fruitful future, and then with the shock of Philippe's untimely death…well, it simply never occurred to me to tell you the truth, until moments ago."

"Surely you'd had opportunity and motive to tell me before now. Why wait?"

"Until now, it didn't matter! Don't you see? Now, without you, St. Michel is in danger of becoming reabsorbed by Rhineland! I had to step forward. As patriots, we simply cannot allow that to happen!"

Sebastian watched her hands clutching and tearing at her hair and dressing gown in a most theatrical fashion. The performance was certainly meant to convince. But could this possibly be true? He did not speak, though thoughts thundered through his mind.

Could he be Philippe de Bergeron's son?

Could this explain the connection he felt to Philippe? The nearly surreal familial bond that had kept him from feeling fatherless at such an early age? Could Philippe have felt some sort of subconscious connection himself? Was that why he'd taken such an interest in Claudette's son? Was that why he'd been so included in palace politics? Given such a position of prestige and power in St. Michel's business world? Was Claudette speaking the truth?

No.

Never.

Then again...

Her story was just left of center enough to be true.

Numb with shock, he tried to reason how this new turn of events could affect his life. He stared at the fire, and watched the flames devour the last of a good-sized chunk of wood. A chill had descended on the room and vaguely, he considered stirring the flames and adding another log. But he was too paralyzed at the moment. Too deep in thought to move.

Not wanting to lose the momentum she'd built, Claudette plunged ahead before he could distract her train of thought.

"Sebastian, my darling, before now, there was no reason to bother you with the sad details of your birth. You were far better off with us. Your...your..." Claudette trumpeted into the wad of tissues she held and bubbles of saliva formed on her lips as she bawled. "Katie died. Most likely of a broken heart. I keep her death certificate and other papers in...in...a safe-deposit box. I haven't seen them in years. It all seems like a..." she waved her tissues, "...dream. You were safe with us. You were our little boy. But now, you are a man. And the very future of the kingdom rests on Philippe's son stepping in and taking the crown. You are crown prince, and, as such, you can save our country from Rhineland, especially since, as far as I know, their marriage was never really annulled!"

She was right on that count.

Overhead an explosion of thunder rattled the windows as Sebastian made a sickening discovery that he suddenly knew was about to ruin his life.

If he was indeed Philippe de Bergeron's son, then he was at the same time Marie-Claire's brother.

Marie-Claire burrowed deep under her feather bed and watched with awe the spectacular storm that had rain sluicing over her windows in sheets. Glowing veins of light branched the sky and thunder boomed in a show that was quite rare for St. Michel.

Especially for March.

She couldn't remember ever having seen anything quite so violent in her twenty-one years in this country. Before now, she'd only read about such things. As the waffled shadow of her French panes flickered on the wall, she wondered how people in less sturdy abodes were faring.

She wondered how Sebastian was faring.

Sebastian.

Nature's wrath only augmented her turbulent feelings since she'd seen him that afternoon. She'd had no idea how powerful their reunion would be for her. When she'd been in Denmark, she'd missed him, to be sure. But just how much became apparent only after he'd liquefied her knees with his kiss.

Eyes closed, she tugged her covers higher and groaned.

Even now she could still feel his warm lips over hers, open, prodding, insistent, his hand around the back of her neck, pulling her closer and she, wilting against him. As they'd stood alone together in the pond that evening, it had been perfect. His kiss had been as warm and wet and sultry as the weather that had rolled in over them.

Fingertips against her mouth, she swallowed a giddy squeal. She was in love. Untamed, stormy, tingling, thrilling love that stole her appetite and robbed her of any rational thought. She couldn't imagine ever feeling more blissful. Happier. More in tune with life.

Though her eyes drifted shut, Marie-Claire knew she'd never be able to sleep. Images of her and Sebastian running for the shore, struggling to pull dry clothing over wet skin, more kissing, riding home just ahead of the storm....

Her earlier worries had seemed light years removed with

his arms around her waist. Only Sebastian knew how to soothe her. To make her chaotic world seem right again. He was the only man for her, and she was sure that he was a gift straight from God himself.

Murmuring to the rhythm of the rain that pelted her windows and balcony, Marie-Claire drew up her knees, clasped her hands beneath her chin and sent up a prayer of thanksgiving for such a perfect match. When she was finished offering her gratitude, she asked the good Lord to tell her Papa not to worry. Everything would eventually work out. Rhineland would drop its ridiculous bid to overtake St. Michel. Her long-lost sibling would be found. Papa's annulment to Katie Graham would be found.

And soon, as all good princesses did, she would marry Sebastian and live happily ever after.

A knock at the door startled Marie-Claire out of a deep, dreamless sleep. She sat up and peered through the darkness to numbers that glowed from her nightstand. Way after midnight. What on earth could anyone want in the wee hours of the morning?

"Just—" She cleared her throat and fumbled for her robe. "Just a minute."

Padding across her room, she pulled open her heavy oak bedroom door and squinted against the shaft of light from the hallway. The security night doorman stood at attention.

"Yes?"

"Your Highness, you have a visitor in the library. Mr. Sebastian LeMarc."

Sebastian? A bubble of joy surged into the back of her throat. It was an effort to maintain a businesslike facade. "Tell him I'll be down in a moment."

"Yes, ma'am."

Marie-Claire rushed to her bathroom, jammed a toothbrush in her mouth, dragged a comb through her hair, spat, fluffed, spritzed, puffed, applied a dash of makeup and finally declared herself ready.

He cut a striking figure, standing in the middle of the massive library, staring at the fire that flickered in the hearth. Before he became aware of her presence, she watched him, and her heart swelled with love.

He was magnificent. Rangy legs spread for balance, he stood, his powerful arms folded over his chest. A long, black trench coat hung to his knees and accentuated the breadth of his shoulders. His hair was damp from the weather and curled most appealingly at his nape and just above his ears. A pensive expression graced his perfectly chiseled mouth, and his gaze was clouded with some unreadable emotion.

Something had happened.

Fear leapt in Marie-Claire's heart. She glanced at the clock that ticked away the hour on the mantle. Nearly two in the morning. What on earth could be wrong?

As if he sensed her presence, Sebastian turned.

The tortured look in his eyes had her flying across the room and finding solace in his embrace. Her hands sought to cup his cheeks and she pulled his mouth to hers, knowing that whatever it was, they could handle it together.

His lips grazed hers and then—oddly—he pulled back. There was stiffness in his countenance that worried Marie-Claire. Eyes flashing, he searched her face and she cast him a tentative smile. She could feel the heat in his hands as he clutched her arms and his breathing came in labored puffs. His hand shook as he traced the barely discernable cleft in her chin with the pad of his thumb.

"In so many ways, you are the feminine version of him."

"Papa?" Marie-Claire's brow furrowed at his strange comment.

"Yes. You have an expression...I don't know...when you smile. It leaves no doubt that you are his."

"Mama would have agreed with you. Although, to her way of thinking, the resemblance was not a compliment." Again, she smiled, hoping to lighten his somber expression.

"It must have been why he favored you."

"What?"

"This resemblance. None of your siblings seem to have inherited so much from him."

"None of us inherited what he'd hoped." Her laughter was dry. Rueful. "The similarities would have been much easier to spot in a son."

"Maybe."

"Sebastian, what is it? Surely you did not come here at this hour to discuss my relationship with my father."

He swallowed and glanced away. "No."

"Then what? You're scaring me."

"I'm sorry." His eyes slid closed and with a heavy exhalation, he rested his head against hers. "I came here to talk to you."

"At this hour, it must be grave."

"I don't know."

"Sebastian, please." Her heart was pounding. Again, he held her apart from his body and scrutinized her face in a most unnerving manner. "Have I done something wrong? Said something?"

"No."

"Then what?"

She lifted a finger and rested it on his lower lip and the simple gesture seemed to scald him. Roughly, he grasped her hand and reared back. Hurt, white-hot in its intensity, crowded into her throat, this simple rejection rendering her speechless.

On the mantle, the clock ticked, and, beneath it, the fire

crackled in the hearth. Outside, the sounds of a dying storm whispered through the trees.

"I have to go." Sebastian released her hand and took a step back. And then, another.

"What? But you just got here. And you needed to talk to me."

"I...no. I was wrong."

His simple words held a deeper nuance that she could not fathom, but she knew that something had happened. Something that would change the course of her life. Marie-Claire suddenly knew a fear of loss that overshadowed the death of her father.

"Now. I have to go now." His eyes were cloudy and almost anguished as he backed toward the door. "Goodbye, Marie-Claire."

Marie-Claire's lungs froze in midbreath.

Good-bye?

Why did this usually breezy parting hold such an echo of permanence? Wordlessly, she watched him stride through the massive palace foyer, past the guards, and out through the several sets of double doors that led to his freedom.

Just outside Sebastian's bedroom window the next morning, the sky was a brilliant blue, showing no sign of last night's freak hurricane. The news had reported damage in the millions and more than a dozen fatalities connected with the unusual spring storm. Now, the sun belied the devastation of the night before and streamed into his room, warming great patches on his bed and the floor. The dust had been settled and the air had a scrubbed-fresh quality that Sebastian usually reveled in.

But not this morning.

This morning, he noticed none of the splendor in the world beyond his window, for he was focused on the cracks in his heart. Woodenly, he forced himself to go through the motions of dressing. Preparing for the day. The day after the world had ended.

He hadn't been able to tell her.

He hated himself for his weakness, but it had been beyond his ability when she was so close. Even forcing himself to leave hadn't helped build his courage. Neither had the whiskey he'd drunk when he'd come home, hoping to lull himself into a forgetful stupor. That stupid stunt had only managed to drive what felt like a rusty ax through his brain, leaving his head pounding, his mouth a dust bowl, and his heart a bloody ball of hamburger.

What the devil was he going to do now?

It seemed his only recourse was to meet with Simone and get to the bottom of this mess. The…truth. Then he'd either continue his path with Marie-Claire, or pick up the pieces and do his duty for his country.

It was that simple.

And that horrible.

Sebastian's hands stilled as he buttoned his collar and stared at his haggard reflection in the full-length mirrored doors of his closet. He hadn't slept a wink all night long for lying there and calling himself every kind of fool. It had been lunacy to see Marie-Claire. He should have known that he had no willpower where she was concerned. Her understanding expression and willingness to soothe him without even knowing the problem only endeared her to him further. Made what had to be done between them—temporarily or permanently—only that much harder.

Bracing his palms on the back of a chair, he hung his throbbing head and, squeezing his eyes shut against the brilliant sunlight, thought over his life. He'd grown up with wealth and privilege. Even his high-powered career in St. Michel's fast-paced world of import/export had been essentially handed to him because of his social status. Although, why on earth such status should have been afforded his mother was a mystery indeed. She was uneducated, brash, charmless.

It was common knowledge that she'd married into her social position. Claudette was a social climber. But her husband was deceased now. And her eccentricities were becoming more pronounced with age. Surely, she had to sense that high society would eventually move on. Without her.

Then again, Claudette lived in a dream world. Blissfully, she ignored her dwindling bank account and the signs that pointed to her eventual economic failure. She craved prominence in St. Michel's upper echelon, needing to see and be seen. Her lower class upbringing was an albatross about her neck that she routinely glossed over, fancying herself—because of her aristocratic marriage—to be above the common folk. After all, her husband had been a royal consort and a count. And her son...

Sebastian's head jerked up and he scrutinized the face that had stared back at him these thirty-two years. Could there be any truth to Claudette's fantastic story? Truth be told, there were certain similarities between him and Philippe. Some physical, but there were other things.

Both loved to golf. To ride horses. In fact, all manner of sport had them more than intrigued. They shared a common sense of humor, a passion for life, and intolerance for stupidity and cruelty. A complete dedication to St. Michel and her politics. A loyalty to the monarchy, to history, to destiny. A belief in God and the power of love.

But did these things add up to a blood relationship?

Claudette swore they did.

Sebastian dragged his hands over his face, rubbing his painful temples and forehead. Knowing Claudette as he did, he knew she was not beyond lying. But he'd never known her to fabricate anything to these lengths.

Even so, until he knew the absolute truth, he had to stay away from Marie-Claire. Should the public catch wind of this rumor and suspect anything deeper in their relationship, it could be catastrophic for everyone involved.

Sebastian dropped into the chair that sat at the end of his bed and reached for his shoes. He allowed a loafer to dangle from his fingertips and stared into the mirror as he mulled over his identity. Just who the hell was he? One day, he was a successful playboy, wooing the king's daughter and the next, he was heir to the throne and was dating his half sister.

Confused didn't begin to describe his state of mind.

Even so, several things were becoming dismally clear. Now that his identity was in question, he was shocked at how he'd allowed the life he'd been handed to dictate who he was.

Well, no more.

Soon enough, Sebastian would find out who his parents really were. And in the process, he hoped, he'd discover exactly who he was. Filled with a sense of purpose, Sebastian jammed his feet into his shoes, shrugged into his coat, and strode to the door.

Time to get to the bottom of this mess. As much as he hated the idea of Marie-Claire learning the truth, he knew that there was no time like the present.

He'd swing by and pick up his mother on the way to the palace.

Chapter Six

As the head of security for St. Michel, Luc Dumont knew he must squelch the urge to squirm under the Dowager Queen Simone's intense scrutiny. Because he'd already been hired by Prime Minister Rene Davoine to locate the missing heir, he knew this interview with Her Royal Highness was simply a formality. Nevertheless, it was nervewracking. His dealings with some of the world's most hardened criminals suddenly seemed a breeze in comparison to this social interrogation.

The old woman sat, shoulders square, hands clasped in her lap, both feet planted firmly on the floor. Over the years, her severe expression had etched censorious creases into the corners of her mouth and between her eyes. And these eyes, like blue laser beams, missed nothing as they bored into his soul.

It was not every day he spent the morning chatting with royalty in the throne room. Especially crotchety, old royalty, poised like a buzzard, ready to pounce and peck away at even the slightest lapse in the dedication of the police to her case. It was times like these that Luc wished he'd gone into sales, like his father before him.

Luckily for him, Simone preferred a comfortable pair of overstuffed chairs in a grouping by the window to the throne itself, which, to his surprise, actually sat on a small stage in the middle of the room. On a low table before them, a tray laden with fresh pastries lay untouched. Luc knew he'd never be able to chew, let alone swallow in front of such unabashed scrutiny. He shifted in his seat, touched his tongue to his dry lips and glanced around the intimidating room. With the exception of the ever-present security people stationed at the far doors, they were alone.

He glanced back at Simone, wondering where to look. Her shoes were very plain. Functional. There seemed to be a bit of tissue stuck to the bottom of one.

"Are you looking at my legs?"

"Wha...what?" Dazed, Luc snapped his head up from his introspective pose and felt every drop of blood in his body rush to his cheeks.

"My legs. You seem to be staring at them." She picked a bit of fluff from her pencil skirt.

"No! No, I was..." The old bird thought he'd been *checking out her legs?* Mortified, his gaze dropped to her legs, which weren't that bad, all things considered— Good heavens man, *don't look at her legs!* He glanced around for a focal point, any focal point, found it in an exit sign and wished he were on the other side.

"Don't be embarrassed, young man. I pride myself on keeping my figure trim."

"But I was just noticing—" Needing vindication, he gestured to the tissue on her shoe, but she paid no heed.

"Daily walks. I can do a fourteen-minute mile. Pretty good for an old broad pushing eighty, don't you think?"

"Yes, but—"

"You look vaguely familiar to me, and I'm not saying that as a pick-up line." Simone stared at him, her dry, rather flirtatious humor at odds with the permanent scowl on her face. "However, I don't believe we've met before today?"

"I—" Because the moment had passed, Luc gave his head a clearing shake and decided to let the leg issue drop. "You may have seen me interviewed on the local news last month, in a case connected with a French smuggling ring."

"Perhaps. Though I'm not much on TV, unless it's that *Iron Chef* thing. You ever see that?" She chuckled, not caring if he answered. "And *The Antiques Road Show*. Oh, and *Biography*. I'm waiting for them to call me anytime now, as my childhood would make a riveting story... At any rate, where were we?"

"Have we met before?" he prompted.

"Are you flirting with me, young man?"

Again, Luc was at a loss, but she seemed not to notice and instead chuckled at her private joke.

"Oh, yes. Now then." Simone gathered her thoughts. "Before you tell me how you plan to find my missing grandchild, tell me a little about yourself. I like to know who I'm working with."

Anxious to get out of there, Luc decided it best to plunge in at the beginning with an abridged version of his thirty-something years.

"I was born in the United States, but grew up in France. My maternal grandparents died when I was four and my mother died when I was six. When my father remarried, I was sent off to study in England. First at Eton and then at Cambridge. The father of a friend of mine at Cambridge suggested that I go for a career in Interpol, which I had for eight years. I was then brought in as head of the Security Force for St. Michel."

"Why?"

The sharp question took Luc off guard. Why indeed? The fact that he felt that he belonged nowhere in particular was hardly the answer of a professional. "Uh, well, because I was qualified."

"And, exactly what is it that qualifies you to find my grandchild?"

"Other than my education and experience?"

Simone issued a curt nod.

Luc shrugged as he pondered his answer. "I think, in this case, it's because I feel a bit of empathy toward your missing heir. He or she lost their father when they were very young. I lost my mother. I spent time living in both the United States and France and have an understanding of both cultures and...I know what it's like to—"

"To what?"

"—to long for family."

Simone's probing stare warmed a degree or two and for a moment there, she looked nearly maternal. Luc bit back a grin. When she was young, he imagined that she'd been a handful. Probably kind of pretty to boot.

"Very well, then. Tell me what you've discovered so far."

Luc swallowed a sigh of relief. Apparently, he'd passed muster. "As of yesterday, we know that Katie Graham gave birth—"

An odd explosion at the far end of the room drew their attention.

The massive mahogany double doors to the throne room flew open and Sebastian LeMarc burst through, pausing only to issue an urgent apology to the understandably agitated security guards. A wailing Claudette trotted at his heels. Arms outstretched and fingers fluttering, she begged him not to cause a scene.

Sebastian rolled his eyes and tossed a feral frown over

his shoulder, willing her to shut up, but it was futile. Claudette was on a roll.

Recognizing Sebastian and his mother as Marie-Claire's sometime special guests, the guards looked to the Dowager Queen. The slight bob of her head gave them permission to relax and resume their posts.

Before meeting with the queen, Sebastian had wanted to stop and speak with Marie-Claire. Unfortunately, Marie-Claire had been indisposed when they arrived and Claudette's highly distraught emotional state would not allow them to tarry.

Perhaps it was better this way.

First, he could meet with Queen Simone and his mother and then talk to Marie-Claire in private, later, when he had all of the facts. She needed to hear about this debacle from him, and in private. Although—Sebastian's jaw tensed at the thought of that tortured conversation—he'd rather face a firing squad than lose the other half of his soul.

Intent on quickly getting to the bottom of this mess, he strode across the room to Simone. In his hands he carried the paperwork Claudette had collected from a friend of a friend who didn't mind going into the government offices at the crack of dawn to collect documents. For a generous fee, of course.

The noisy interruption tugged Queen Simone's lips down at the corners. "*Mis*ter LeMarc, what is the meaning of this unscheduled visit?"

"I beg Your Highness's forgiveness in this terrible breach of etiquette, but some important information has suddenly come to light that I think you will find most interesting."

Diamonds flashing, Simone waved her spotty, blue-veined hands about and made proper introductions. "Sebastian LeMarc, I'd like you to meet Luc Dumont, head of St.

The Silhouette Reader Service™ — Here's how it works:

If offer card is missing write to: Silhouette Reader Service, 3010 Walden Ave., P.O. Box 1867, Buffalo NY 14240-1867

NO POSTAGE
NECESSARY
IF MAILED
IN THE
UNITED STATES

BUSINESS REPLY MAIL
FIRST-CLASS MAIL   PERMIT NO. 717-003   BUFFALO, NY

POSTAGE WILL BE PAID BY ADDRESSEE

SILHOUETTE READER SERVICE
3010 WALDEN AVE
PO BOX 1867
BUFFALO NY 14240-9952

Play The Lucky Hearts Game

and get...
FREE BOOKS & a FREE GIFT...
YOURS to KEEP!

Scratch Here!
then look below to see
what your cards get you...

Yes! I have scratched off the silver card. Please send me my **2 FREE BOOKS** and **FREE GIFT**. I understand that I am under no obligation to purchase any books as explained on the back of this card.

315 SDL DH4C   **215 SDL DH4A**

NAME   (PLEASE PRINT CLEARLY)

ADDRESS

APT.#   CITY

STATE/PROV.   ZIP/POSTAL CODE

Twenty-one gets you
2 FREE BOOKS and
a **FREE GIFT!**

Twenty gets you
2 FREE BOOKS!

Nineteen gets you
1 FREE BOOK!

TRY AGAIN!

Offer limited to one per household and not valid to current Silhouette Romance® subscribers. All orders subject to approval.

Visit us online at
www.eHarlequin.com

Michel's Security Force. Luc, the red-faced woman snivel-
ing behind him is Claudette LeMarc, Sebastian's mother.''

Knees popping, Claudette bobbed in an awkward curtsey.

Sebastian took Luc's proffered hand. ''Please, forgive my
intrusion, but I believe I might save you both some valuable
time.''

''Go on.''

''I have reason to believe that you can dismiss Mr. Dumont—my sincere apologies, sir—as the missing heir is no
longer…missing.''

Simone stiffened. ''I do not take kindly to word games,
LeMarc. If you have an heir, produce him. Now.''

''I have, Your Highness.'' Sebastian glanced without
sympathy at his mother, who looked ready to faint. ''Apparently, you are looking at him.''

Marie-Claire stood in the doorway, not sure that she'd
heard correctly. Sebastian's words hung in the air, flash-
freezing the group by the window into a tableau of shock
and wonder.

Sebastian was claiming to be the missing heir?

Her brow creased as she puzzled over this odd announcement.

Why had he never told her this before? And, if he were
the missing heir, wouldn't that make him crown prince?
And, if he was the crown prince, wouldn't that make him
Philippe's son with an American woman named Katie
Something-or-other? And, if he was Philippe's son wouldn't
that make him—

As she staggered into the throne room, Marie-Claire's
ears began to buzz. Her face caught fire and the bile rose
in her throat. Okay. She was going to faint. She groped
about for something, anything to keep her upright, but there

was nothing. Only sparkling, shimmering air and swirling walls.

At the door one of the guards glanced at her with concern. Her weak smile and glazed expression had him rushing to her side to offer his assistance. Marie-Claire fought the wave of hysterical laughter that threatened to run amok. She must look quite insane. She certainly felt that way. Although the throne was normally off-limits to anyone but the king himself, the guard led her to it, as clearly, this was a special occasion. Upon arriving at the garish gold and bejeweled chair, she fell most gracelessly upon the velvet cushion and did battle with the urge to vomit. Head between her knees, pasty face cradled in clammy palms she listened as across the room, the stunned dowager found her voice.

"*You* are Philippe and Katie's son?" Simone stared first at Sebastian, then at his mother. "Claudette? How could this be true?"

Claudette stumbled forward and sank without invitation to a seat near the queen. Head bowed, hands clasped beneath her chin, she assumed an ingratiating position. "I...I...was there. At the wedding." She turned her watery gaze to Luc. "Look it up. You will see it's true."

Though suspicion marred his expression, Luc nodded. "This much is true. The signature of a Claudette LeMarc is on the wedding license as a witness."

Again, the room fell silent for a moment as everyone digested this startling turn of events. Marie-Claire allowed herself a miserable peek and seeing Sebastian standing there, so handsome, so strong, so regal—

She ducked her head back into her lap to shut out the horrible image of him as her possible brother.

"Sebastian," Queen Simone barked and pointed, "do sit down. You're making me quite nervous. Would anyone care for a cup of coffee? Perhaps something stronger? It's early," her expression was wry, "but I could use a cocktail about now. Or perhaps an IV drip of something poisonous." Soundlessly, a young servant girl moved to pour coffee.

Her dry wit pushed a small smile to his lips as Sebastian moved to take the empty seat on Simone's other side.

China rattling, Claudette accepted her cup of coffee with shaking hands. "She couldn't keep him."

"Pardon?" Simone stared with undisguised distaste at the overwrought Claudette and her roundabout way of reaching the point.

"Katie and Philippe were told by someone in authority that their marriage was not legal."

The old queen glanced from Claudette to the floor and had the grace to color ever so slightly.

"Katie could not face going home and subjecting her poor child to the shame of being born out of wedlock. So, she stayed with my husband and me in France for seven and a half months, until the baby was born. Then, after..." Claudette paused to honk into her handkerchief before she was able to continue, "after a heart-rending decision, she left him in our care."

Simone exhaled and peered over the rim of her glasses, pensive thoughts drawing her fine brows together. Slowly, her head moved from side to side. "I can scarcely believe that Philippe would never have confided this part of the story to me."

"Because he did not know! Katie's father told Philippe that she had left the country and that the baby was to be adopted out to an American family. Philippe was but a child himself. He had no experience. No recourse." Lost in her tortured reverie, Claudette stared out the window in a dramatic pose, searching her memory for the finer points of the story.

"Do go on," Simone ordered, growing impatient with the theatrics.

"My husband and I were childless at the time. As aristocrats, closely affiliated with royalty," she tilted her chin back and sniffed, "Katie felt that we were the perfect parents for her child, imbued with the proper pedigree with which to give her son everything she could not. Needless to say, we were overjoyed at the prospect of finally becoming parents. Shortly after the birth, we filed for adoption—" She blinked at Luc. "Sir, you may make copies of the legal paperwork I have uncovered and brought with me today."

"You can be sure I will."

"Yes. Yes. Of course." A bright smile stretched across her teeth, and quickly fell away as she continued with her story. "Katie then returned to Texas to resume life with her father. Several years later, my husband and I moved to St. Michel with Sebastian and raised him as our own. Philippe never knew that Sebastian was his son."

Marie-Claire leapt to her feet, swung off the throne and staggered dizzily across the room, one hand outstretched, one cupping her aching head. "*No!* No, I don't believe it. She's *lying!* This cannot be true! Sebastian, don't believe her!"

"Marie-Claire?" Sebastian snapped around at the sound of her voice. The life seemed to leak from his being as his head fell back and his eyes slid closed.

"It's *not true,* I'm telling you," she shouted. "Claudette." Marie-Claire turned on the older woman. Claudette stared warily up at her. "Why are you *doing this?*"

"I'm sorry if this news unsettles you, my dear, but it is the truth."

"I—" Marie-Claire opened her mouth to argue, but was interrupted by yet another tortured shriek.

"*No!*" All heads—including Marie-Claire's—swung to

the far door as this piercing scream reverberated from ceiling to wall and back again. Borne on fury, Celeste swept across the room. The veins bulged at her slender throat and her fists bunched at her sides, poised to strike.

"This," Celeste shrieked and pointed at Claudette, "is outrageous! Are you going to believe this…this…social-climbing *maggot?*"

Affronted, Claudette gasped. "How *dare*—"

"Shut up!" Celeste's hostile gaze swung to Queen Simone. "You *dotty old bat!* There is *no…missing…heir!*"

As the fractious hubbub ensued, Marie-Claire wanted—for the first time ever—nothing more than to believe her father's hateful widow.

Rushing to investigate the commotion from where they'd been brunching in the salon down the hall, Lise and Ariane appeared, followed by Georges and Juliet. Upon learning the latest, their voices rose and the chaos escalated. Soon, everyone was hurling recriminations and casting aspersions in a free-for-all.

Sebastian climbed upon the pastry table and with steely eyes, surveyed the pandemonium. *"Silence!"*

Everyone, the dowager queen included, froze at his command. Not a sound could be heard as he stood, hands on hips, eyes glittering, muscles working in his jaw.

An eon seemed to pass before he spoke again, and when he did, his voice was dangerously low. All eyes focused on him, and everyone, whether they wanted to admit it or not, wondered if they were truly hearing from the crown prince, for he certainly fit the part.

"I have never wanted to be a prince, let alone king. I have no desire whatsoever to fill the position now, or ever. I am as stunned by this sudden revelation as the rest of you."

He turned his gaze upon Marie-Claire for a long, sorrow-filled moment, and the tension radiated between them, causing eyebrows to lift.

With a valiant effort, Marie-Claire attempted to stem the tide of her emotion, but it was useless. Tears streamed down her cheeks. She would never, ever buy into this pack of lies that Claudette was foisting upon her own flesh and blood.

Marie-Claire's gaze flashed between Claudette and Sebastian.

Was she the only one who saw the familial resemblance? The same thick, wavy dark hair, the same slight cleft in the chin, the same cobalt eyes, the same strong jaw. She turned her attention to Claudette—loathing the woman who was attempting to ruin her life—and squinted. Thankfully, physical appearance was where the resemblance between mother and son ended.

Claudette was a swirling mass of insecurities and self-doubt. Her son, on the other hand, was the complete antithesis. Where Claudette was weak, Sebastian was strong. Where Claudette was cloying and manipulative, Sebastian was forthright and honest. Where Claudette needed the approval of others, Sebastian was secure in his own skin.

Her gaze traveled to Sebastian's and locked. Silently, Marie-Claire implored him to come to his senses.

He stared at her, reading her mind, anguishing with her, but unable, for many reasons, to do her bidding. Finally, he tore his glance away, destroying her heart in the process.

"Luc," Sebastian said, "I want you to investigate further into this matter. Find out what you can about my..." he shot a look of derision at Claudette, "...*real* parents, whoever they are. And, Your Highness," he turned to Simone, "I will leave the next step in this calamity to your discretion and to the royal protocol regarding such matters."

Simone nodded.

Marie-Claire stared.

Celeste shrieked.

Once again, all hell broke loose.

Sick to death of the bickering, Sebastian strode out of the room.

Marie-Claire caught up with Sebastian where the corridor ended at the top of one of the four different fantastic de Bergeron Palace staircases. Breathless, she called to him, and it was only the desperation in her voice that halted his rapid escape.

The banister supported his weight as he stopped and turned to face her, even though it was the last thing he wanted to do. Knowing what they had shared together and knowing that there was the possibility—however slight— that she could be his half sister, nauseated him. Heartsick, and suddenly very ill at ease in her presence, he took a deep breath and unwillingly met her eyes with his own. He tried not to flinch as she reached out to touch his arm.

"Sebastian." Lips quivering, her smile was filled with uncertainty.

"What?"

"Surely, you don't believe this crazy story."

The air whooshed from his lungs at her pitiful plea. It took a Herculean effort to stand so near and yet not reach for her. He rubbed his aching head and stared over her shoulder to the wall.

"Why not? She has proof. Legal documents." He snorted derisively. "I'm the right age and there is no denying that there are other similarities—"

"Coincidence!"

He shook his head. "Marie-Claire, don't."

"Sebastian—"

"Marie-Claire, you have to admit there might be a grain of truth to all of this."

"Never!"

"You can't say that. I wouldn't put it past Claudette to have lied to me all these years. Though she is a loving mother, she is basically selfish."

"Exactly! Which is why *she is lying now!*" Marie-Claire moved to stand against him and, with the ornate railing at his back, there was no escaping her touch. She grasped the placket of his shirt and pressed her wet cheek against his chest. Hot tears scalded his flesh and her voice came in muffled bursts. "This cannot be happening."

His arms at his sides, Sebastian stood helplessly as she wept, her body quaking with emotion. Torn and miserable, he did battle with himself and willed her not to cry.

But she did. Pitiful, body-wracking sobs that jarred him to his very soul. She swiped at her tears with the edges of her hands, and tried valiantly to pull herself together, only to have the pain escape again in great gasps of sorrow that echoed throughout the cavernous marble hall.

Sebastian closed his eyes, feeling the lump of lead in his own throat swell to unbearable proportions, cutting off his oxygen, leaving him impossibly weak where she was concerned. He wished he could say something, anything, to take away her agony, but there were no words.

She continued to sob against his chest, clutching his shirt to keep from falling to her knees.

Knowing he must hold her or die, Sebastian circled her waist with his arms and pulled her tight. "Marie-Claire," he murmured into her hair, savoring the taste of her precious name on his lips. "Marie-Claire, please, don't cry, sweetheart."

The endearment seemed to shatter her and she clutched him ever closer.

He ran his hands up her back, filled his hands with her

hair and, cupping her head, tilted her face back, and kissed her mottled cheeks.

"Please, Sebastian." Eyes flashing, she beseeched him. "Don't let this happen. Please believe me when I tell you that Claudette is lying. What mother withholds this kind of information for thirty-two years?"

"What good would this knowledge have done me?"

"Sebastian, she sees opportunity."

"Maybe." He wished he could be completely sure that she was right. But he couldn't. Not yet. Perhaps not ever. "Maybe not. But no matter what the outcome, Marie-Claire, this has put us both in an extremely awkward situation. Especially with the press."

"To hell with the press! I'm sick of the public running my life."

"No, Marie-Claire, think about it from the public's point of view. Lovers, or siblings? Or even worse, *both?* News of our relationship and this birth scandal could cause no end of heartache to everyone involved until we sort out the truth."

Marie-Claire buried her face in his shirt and a keening wail came from deep within her soul. *"No-o."*

He wanted to die.

"Oh, Marie-Claire." He held her tight, cradling her in his arms, rubbing her back and rocking her as he would a small, frightened child. "Marie-Claire, no matter what, I care far too much for you," he swallowed against the grief that burned, "and your father, to ever take a chance on hurting you with this."

"But you are!" She reared back and stared up at him, her gaze imploring. "Sebastian, it's simply not possible that you are my brother! Don't you see? You are a gift from God to me! We were made for each other! We belong together, not as brother and sister, but as husband and wife!"

As much as it tortured him, Sebastian knew it was up to him to be strong. "Marie-Claire, right now, I don't even know who I am."

"I do."

"Tell me."

"The other half of me."

His own words came back to haunt him as she quoted what he'd told her just yesterday. On impulse, Marie-Claire pressed her mouth to his, and for a moment, Sebastian lost all rational thought, his heart tumbling with an avalanche of forbidden desire. Marie-Claire was persistent, pressing his lips open with her own, warming his cheeks with her breath, nipping, tasting, urging.

It was too intense.

"No."

Fearing that he might be losing himself in his sister's kiss, he thrust her roughly away and—heart hammering, breath coming in labored puffs—took several steps down the stairs.

Clutching the balustrade, Marie-Claire sank to her knees.

"We can't do this, Marie-Claire. We can't." Without daring a backward glance, Sebastian left her sobbing at the top of the stairs.

Chapter Seven

It had been twenty-four hours.

Just enough crying time to bruise Marie-Claire's usually peachy complexion and swell her almond-shaped eyes to veritable walnuts. A demonic dance troop had taken up residence in her brain, fox-trotting on her temples and doing the rumba on her eardrums. She knew she needed an aspirin or two, or perhaps—heavy sigh—a dozen, and would have slogged into her bathroom to find some, if she could only be sure she'd live long enough for them to take effect.

Outside her window, a tiny songbird landed on her sill and proceeded to serenade her with its lyrical warble.

"Oh...*shut up!*" she moaned and flopped about in her bed until she located a decorative pillow and flung it at the pane.

Life was over.

She had no reason to go on. She'd lost her one true love and the color had eked from her existence, leaving her emotionally monochromatic.

Black.

White.

And shades of eternal, dismal…

Gray.

A long, unrepressed hiss leaked from between her lips. Her eyes slid shut and she clutched her head as the nightmare of yesterday morning's hideous proclamation revisited. Claudette's shrill voice reverberated in the back of her brain, crying *"He's Philippe's son,"* over and over, and driving Marie-Claire half mad with panic.

After Sebastian had left, she'd sped to her suite, locking herself inside and refusing to eat or drink or speak to anyone, sending family and servant alike away to wonder and worry. She had no desire to eat. To drink. To speak.

Why bother?

Everyone, with the lone exception of herself, had bought into a ridiculous lie. For the love of St. Michel, they need only look at Claudette to see the blessed truth. They were *blood-related.* The town idiot could have figured out that much.

All right, so King Philippe had also had mesmerizing blue eyes and a tiny cleft in the chin.

So what?

And, yes, a little dimple too, and perhaps the same silver-tinged dark hair. And…that resonating vocal timbre that Marie-Claire loved so well in both of them, but that did *not* make him Sebastian's father.

Did it?

No!

"No, no, *no!*" Marie-Claire scraped a knuckle beneath her eyes and pressed her mouth to the satin hem of her blanket. *Sebastian was not her brother!*

They were meant to be lovers. Mates. Parents together. Fate would not be so cruel.

With the speed and dexterity of a three-legged tortoise,

Marie-Claire threw back her covers, dragged herself to a sitting position and surveyed her shocking reflection in the vanity mirror across the room. A poster child for "America's Most Wanted" stared back at her. Her hair stood away from her head like the great, tangled dreads of a shedding golden retriever. Black circles, one part mascara, two parts anguish, circled her red-rimmed eyes and her face appeared to have—she leaned closer and squinted—tire tracks imbedded in her cheeks, no doubt from having been run over by a pack of lies.

Cold and stiff as rigor mortis, Marie-Claire slowly scooted to the edge of her massive canopied bed, and sat for a moment to catch her breath from the exertion.

A knock at the door set the cranial demons to dancing again.

"Go away."

"Marie-Claire, honey, we are concerned. Please. Let us in."

She could hear Lise and Ariane whispering in the hallway.

"Go away." No way was she up for the double dose of sisterly pity that waited.

"We have cinnamon rolls and coffee."

Marie-Claire sat up a little straighter. Then again, some sympathy might be just what the doctor ordered. She stumbled to the door, fiddled with locks and yanked it open.

Her sisters gasped at the grim reaper incarnate standing before them and, with a roll of her bloodshot eyes, Marie-Claire waved them inside and staggered back to bed.

"She looks like Jonah after the whale spewed him out," Ariane observed.

"Should we call the doctor?" Lise wondered.

"Stop talking about me as if I'm not here."

Lise bustled to the window, pushed back the blackout

drapes and threw open the windows to freshen the stale air.
Ariane set down a tray, poured Marie-Claire a steaming mug
of coffee, then grabbed a brush and sitting down on the bed,
began working out her sister's tangles.

"Ouch!"

"Too hot?"

"No, you're tearing my hair out of my head."

"Sorry."

"So." In the shaft of light that now flooded the room,
Lise turned and smoothed her hands over her crisp slacks.
At only three months pregnant, she still had no need of
maternity wear. "It's a broken heart, I see."

Marie-Claire cast a droll look at her sister. "What was
your first clue?"

Smiling sadly, Lise joined Ariane and perched at the edge
of the bed. "Sometimes it takes an older sister some time
to realize that her baby sister is all grown up and capable
of such deep emotion."

"I'll say," Ariane groused.

"I'm still waiting for *you* to grow up," Lise retorted.

"I beg your pardon? Just because you're married you
seem to think that you can impart advice on all subj—"

"Don't blame my marriage for the fact that you won't
mature—"

"Uh... Excuse me?" Marie-Claire stared back and forth
between her sisters. "Could we please focus on *my* problems for once?"

Suddenly contrite, they nodded. From Lise, "Of course,
Marie-Claire. What can we do to help?"

Jaw set with determination, Marie-Claire puckered her
lips and blew at the steam rising from her mug. "I need
your best advice on how to win a man's attention."

"Would this man be..." Lise placed a flat palm against
her chest and swallowed, "...Sebastian?"

"Duh."

"Our new big brother, Sebastian?" Ariane stared at her agog.

"Yes."

"You want to win the affections of a man that could be...our...our..." As if she were trying to expel an olive pit, Lise pursed her mouth against this assault on her delicate sensibilities. *"...brother?* Marie-Claire, honey, that's just plain—"

"Gross!" Ariane supplied.

"He's *not our brother!*"

"You can't know that for sure," Lise told her.

"Yes! I do!"

"How?"

"Gut instinct, sixth sense, I don't know! Women's intuition! Call it what you will." With her free hand, Marie-Claire gripped the rails at the end of her bed and hauled herself to her knees, tilting her mug at a dangerous angle. Animation chased the fatigue from her features. "Watch his mother's eyes when she talks about adopting him from Katie. A mother's eyes cannot lie. Sebastian is her birth son."

"But what reason could Claudette possibly have for saying he's her adopted son?"

Marie-Claire snorted. "Hello? Crown prince?" Wild gesticulations sent her coffee sloshing over her hands. "Oww." She set the mug back on the tray and sucked the suddenly rising welt on her thumb. "I think Claudette sees herself as some kind of step-dowager-mum-person. I bet she's got her tiara all picked out and everything."

"But Marie-Claire, surely Sebastian can see that she is lying?" Ariane said.

"I think he does."

"Then why is he going along with her?"

"Think, Ariane! She has planted a seed of doubt in everyone. If there is even the remotest possibility that he is my half brother, he knows that our relationship could ruin us both. He would step away from me, even if he knew Claudette was lying, just to protect me."

Lise and Ariane gave this angle some serious consideration and Lise admitted, "I've seen Claudette from time to time down at the country club with her cronies. She *is* a bit of a name dropper."

Ariane said, "And Sebastian shares her startlingly blue eyes. A different hue, really, than Papa's were."

"Now that you mention it, I do see a certain familial resemblance between Sebastian and Claudette."

"It's about time," Marie-Claire groused.

"And it is quite odd that she would wait until now to unveil Sebastian as Papa's son. Why wouldn't she have told him all this before, if it were really true?" Lise stared out the window, pondering.

"Opportunity. Before now, there was none." Marie-Claire's head swiveled back and forth between her sisters. They were beginning to see the light. Even so, Lise was ever practical.

"But what if you are wrong?"

"*I'm not!* Will you trust me on this? Sebastian is no more a member of this family than...than..." she pointed to Lise, "Wilhelm!"

"True." Lise's tone was dry.

"Sorry, honey, I didn't mean it that way."

"I know."

"Anyway, Claudette is up to no good. Don't ask me how I know, I just do. She's the type who will say anything to get what she wants. And she wants power."

"Prestige." Ariane agreed.

"Position." Lise agreed, too.

"We can't let her get away with this. I have to do something. Now! And I need your help. She is ruining my life. And Sebastian's."

"You are really very much in love." Lise reached out and lightly stroked Marie-Claire's hand. A poignant look of longing flashed behind her eyes and was gone.

"Yes."

"Then you cannot chance losing it."

"No," Marie-Claire whispered, aching for her older sister. It would seem that Lise's love life would be next on their "to-fix" list.

Marie-Claire studied her sisters and could tell that they were finally on board and believed, as she did, that Claudette was double-dealing her son's history for personal gain. Gratitude for them both welled, prodding a bubble of joy to rise in her chest. Besides, they both knew that once she set her sights on something, it was far easier to join in on her wacky schemes than to try and beat them.

"I'll help," Lise said on a sigh.

"Me, too."

"Okay." For the first time in twenty-four hours, Marie-Claire grinned. She crawled to the nightstand and found a pad of paper and a pen in the drawer. "You guys talk, I'll take notes. Lise, you have a man. You go first."

A slight grimace graced Lise's face. Marie-Claire darted a concerned peek at Ariane who returned it with one of her own. Even the news of her pregnancy hadn't seemed to draw Wilhelm any closer to his wife.

They watched as Lise tapped her chin with a forefinger and blinked away her melancholy. "Uh...well, I should try to make myself as desirable as possible, I guess."

Marie-Claire began writing. "Desirable. Check." She rubbed the end of the pen against her lower lip. "How?"

Lise wrinkled her nose. "I'd begin by taking a bath."

''Funny. What else?''

''A makeover might be fun. Distracting if nothing else. Why don't we make a day of it, sometime? In Paris? New hair, the latest clothes, the works. For all of us.'' She looked eager and not just for Marie-Claire's sake.

''Hmm. Yes. That's good. Okay. Makeover. Check. If I can get appointments for tomorrow, you're saying that you'll both go with me?''

Lise lifted a dainty shoulder. ''I'd love to. Wilhelm is out of town again and I have nothing better to do.''

Again, Marie-Claire and Ariane exchanged worried glances.

Ariane said, ''I can go. I need to go shopping anyway. I'm planning a little vacation and I've already made a list. Count me in.''

''Okay. Where are you off to?'' Marie-Claire asked as she made herself a note to call the hairdresser. When Ariane didn't immediately answer, she looked up. ''Ariane?''

Ariane gave an artless shrug. ''Rhineland.''

''*Rhineland?*'' Ever maternal, Lise clutched her bosom. ''Whatever for?''

''I've been invited.''

Marie-Claire stared. ''By whom?''

''Etienne.''

''*Etienne?*'' Lise gasped.

''Prince Etienne Kroninberg of Rhineland, *that* Etienne?'' Marie-Claire blinked. ''Etienne the enemy?''

Ariane nodded.

''Are you *insane?*''

''No more so than you.''

''Touché.'' Smile wry, Marie-Claire asked, ''When are you going?''

''I'm leaving Sunday morning.''

''Sunday? But this is already Friday. Why so soon?''

Marie-Claire and Lise watched their sister color.

"I prefer not to discuss it yet."

Marie-Claire glanced at Lise and whispered, "She prefers not to discuss it."

"We are chopped liver."

"I spill my guts to her about my innermost thoughts and feelings, yet she prefers not to discuss hers."

"We can't be trusted."

"Will you both put a lid on it?" Ariane's mouth quirked in annoyance.

"Sure." Marie-Claire feigned a deep emotional wound. "We don't care what you are doing with Etienne."

"Not in the least." Lise also pouted.

"Good."

"Great. Now then. Ariane, since you will be eloping this week with Etienne, what about some advice from you?"

"I'm not eloping!"

"Whatever."

Ariane rested the brush in her lap and tugged at some of the golden strands caught in the bristles. "I don't know. Why don't you ask Sebastian?"

Mouth twisted in disbelief, Marie-Claire cocked her head. As she spoke, sarcasm oozed. "Oh, that's brilliant."

"I'm serious." There was a gleam of mischief in Ariane's eye. "Treat him like a brother. That's what he says he wants, isn't it? If it were me, I'd confide all my juicy secrets in my 'big brother.' Ask his advice on things like dating and what men look for in a woman and what kind of perfume they prefer and where you might find a new boyfriend—"

For a contemplative moment, Marie-Claire stared at her sister, digesting, and then fell back on the bed and her gleeful hoot bounced off the high ceiling. "Oh, Ariane, that *is* brilliant!"

"Take note then, as I have a number of ideas for you."

* * *

Sebastian pulled his Peugeot into his usual spot at the de Bergeron Palace and set the brake. He considered removing his sunglasses, but then thought better of it. The dark circles beneath his eyes were a testament to his sleepless night. This morning, he'd added a lifetime of church and repentance to his "to-do" list because if hell was even half as bad as this last twenty-four hours, he wanted no part of it.

He'd heard through her sisters that Marie-Claire had sequestered herself, refusing to eat or drink or speak to anyone and that had him worried. That, and the fact that she'd ignored his countless phone calls of apology for the way she'd discovered the shocking truth.

Or the shocking pack of lies.

He unfastened his safety belt and stared up through his tinted windshield at her window. Just as soon as he'd attended the emergency meeting that Simone had called this morning—to put a plan of action together for future announcements and to come up with a politically correct spin on his somewhat mystifying ascension to the crown—Sebastian planned on forcing Marie-Claire to answer her door.

Whether she wanted to or not, they eventually had to talk. To figure out their game plan, when it came to talking to the press. When it came to treating each other with careful dignity whenever they were in the public eye together. When it came to surviving the black cloud of devastation that seemed to have settled in his gut and left him feeling like a walking corpse.

He knew she felt the same way.

Maybe, somehow, they could bring some measure of comfort to each other. Sebastian groaned and propped his elbows on his steering wheel and wondered when he'd taken this left turn into eternal damnation.

The sound of voices had him opening an eye and peering out of his tortured reverie.

Two parking spots down, Luc Dumont had just arrived and was greeting the shy Juliet, Philippe's stepdaughter. She looked to be on her way out to run errands. They were smiling and laughing and conversing, as if the very sun hadn't been snuffed out only hours ago.

Sebastian scowled.

Didn't they realize that this dump of a planet had stopped revolving? Bring on the global warming. Use aerosol cans. Stop recycling. Buy a box of Blubber Helper and have the whales for lunch. Why not? Nothing mattered anymore.

Nothing.

Sebastian disembarked and trudged toward the guest entry to check in. Behind him, his car squawked as he shot the locks with his remote. With a brief nod and an exhausted grunt, he acknowledged both Luc and Juliet and absently wondered how the bookish Juliet knew Luc. He could feel them watching him as he moved and decided he'd better get used to it.

Very soon, the world would be watching every move he made.

Marie-Claire watched Sebastian get out of his car from behind the curtains where she sat perched on her bedroom's window seat. At the sight of his handsome face, her heart went into a free fall. Craning her neck, she followed his rangy stride with her eyes, drinking in the sight, memorizing the little details; the way the sun mellowed his usually coffee mane to a deep honey color, the fluid animal-like way of his gait, the blatant masculinity he so unconsciously exuded, the powerful self-possession that made people stop and stare.

As Luc and Juliet were now.

Cheek resting on the back of her hand, Marie-Claire's thoughts traveled back to that morning after her sisters had left so that she could dress. That she hadn't mustered the wherewithal to pick out an outfit was beside the point.

Within moments of Lise and Ariane's departure, she'd overheard Francie, Ariane's gossip-mongering, addle-brained, man-eating—and these were her better qualities—lady-in-waiting, out in the hall regaling several of the chambermaids in a most conspiratorial, "in-the-know" tone, with big news.

"—and a press conference has been called here at the palace for tomorrow night. They say it's to calm fears that Rhineland is on the verge of overtaking St. Michel. But, I think the *real* reason is to cover up a big secret."

"What?" The breathless chambermaids were hanging on Francie's every word.

"Promise you won't say anything to anyone?"

Marie-Claire rolled her eyes.

"We promise. Yes, of course."

"Well, all right. You know I'm dating one of Simone's security guards? Well, *he* said that *Sebastian LeMarc* is…*Philippe's son!*"

A guttural groan welled in Marie-Claire's throat. With Francie on the job the news would spread like greased fire.

"*And,*" Francie gushed, "I'm also dating the son of Simone's personal assistant, and *he* says, until they can figure out how to tell the world, they are using the Rhineland take-over thing as a distraction to keep the paparazzi away. Can you believe it? Sebastian LeMarc as…" the harebrained Francie paused for dramatic effect, then shrieked, "*the crown prince!*"

"*Eeeeee!*" The high pitch of their cries surely had St. Michel's canine set yowling in harmony.

"*Isn't he fabulous?*"

Just beyond her door, Marie-Claire heard the ecstatic cavorting of happy feet.

She was going to be sick.

Nevertheless, she couldn't seem to tear herself away from this morbid fascination she had with learning more of Sebastian's future.

Francie was only too delighted to fill in the missing details. "Plus, another man I am dating from the kitchen crew—"

Marie-Claire stared in wonder at the door. Was there anyone on the staff that Francie was *not* dating?

"—*he* says that this morning, Simone is meeting with her secretary, a slew of press and political advisors, the prime minister, Rene Davoine, and *Sebastian LeMarc*—"

"*Eeeeee!*" the groupie maids couldn't contain their glee. "George Clooney's better-looking little brother will be living *here*," one of them screeched.

"Yes! And," the man-hungry Francie went on, "they've hired Luc Dumont, some cute guy from St. Michel security who I'd like to get my hands on. Is this the most exciting thing to hit St. Michel in years, or what?"

"*Eeeeee!*"

"There will be a big party in the Crystal Ballroom immediately following tomorrow night's press conference, to celebrate St. Michel's continued independence from Rhineland. Everyone who's anyone will be there."

Their hysterical hubbub told Marie-Claire that they all hoped to be called upon to work this party, as it was sure to go down in history as St. Michel's finest hour. Marie-Claire's head thunked against the door, scattering the magpies in the hall.

It had taken her several hours and a half bottle of antacid to recover from that blow.

The double squawk of Sebastian's Peugeot locking

snapped Marie-Claire from her morose ruminations and back to the present.

This "pre-press conference" meeting, she decided, must be the reason he was there. A raw yearning filled her belly as she watched him nod at Juliet, and then disappear into the palace.

Her gaze drifted back to her reserved stepsister, and Marie-Claire briefly wondered what she had to chat about with that guy from security. Marie-Claire knew that Juliet was spending some time comforting their young half sister, Jacqueline. But beyond that…a twinge of guilt niggled because of what she didn't know about Juliet. Really, the woman was so shy and bookish, one scarcely noticed whether she was present or not.

Marie-Claire watched as Luc handed her stepsister into her car, closed her door, then leaned against it and continued to visit through the open window.

Hmm.

Luc hadn't seemed convinced that Claudette was telling the truth yesterday, either. With a thumbnail, Marie-Claire rubbed the edge of her lip. Perhaps she should meet with him, and compare notes.

Perhaps Juliet could introduce them.

Marie-Claire's eyes narrowed. Was he probing Juliet for information? Or was he flirting? Marie-Claire couldn't imagine Juliet flirting with anyone, let alone a sophisticated, rather mature guy like Luc Dumont. She couldn't help but feel a little bit sorry for Juliet, and hoped that she didn't go and do something stupid like fall in love with an older man.

A handsome older man.

A handsome older man who might turn out to be some damned member of the family…

With a grimace, Marie-Claire pushed off the window seat and back onto the floor where she'd been sprawled all afternoon doing "homework" of sorts. Armed with a pile of pillows, a bowl of popcorn, a pitcher of lemonade, a stack of fashion magazines, library books, genealogy websites, nail polish, cotton balls, a television remote control and a notepad and pen, she'd been digging like an archeology student during dead week.

And it was hard work, this. She'd already spent some time on the Internet, reviewing what she could find of Claudette's history, researching the subject of pathological liars—Claudette fit the profile to a T—and trying to find something, anything on a woman named Katie Graham who'd fallen in love with her father, thirty-three years ago.

Since she'd run into some dead ends, she decided to change tack and concentrate on her quest to help Sebastian see that she was the woman for him.

Aiming the remote, she turned the sound back up on the television. As far as she was concerned, the Americans cornered the market on pushy sexuality. At Ariane's prompting, she'd begun her studies with American TV that very morning and would branch out to other cultures, once she got some answers.

So far, she'd flipped through several hundred cable networks making notes here and there, and she had just now landed on *The Jerry Springer Show*. Leaning forward, she peered at the screen to decipher today's topic. A jolt of excitement skittered down her spine as she realized that—oddly enough—the subject was: Men who have married their cousins, and the women who love them.

Microphone in hand, Jerry spun to face his first guest, a Mrs. Lula Parnell, twenty-eight-year-old mother of seven. Marie-Claire stared at the poor thing in astonishment. Gracious sakes, the woman looked *eighty*-eight.

Jerry glanced at his note cards and then affected a sympathetic expression. "Lula, you married your first cousin,

Junior Parnell, when you were thirteen years of age. Is that correct?''

"Yessiree. Thirteen and a half, actually. He was full-grel, though, and already out of the fifth grade.''

"Together, you and Junior have seven children?''

"And a little bun in the oven.'' Lula gave her tummy a maternal pat.

"Junior is unaware that you are pregnant?''

"He's gonna find out right here, on your show.''

"Yes. Junior is waiting backstage with his current wife and stepsister, Ona.''

The veins in Lula's neck suddenly bulged. "Yessir. That *bleeeep* stole my *bleeeeping* man from me and when I get my hands on that *bleeping bleep,* I'll *bleep* her *bleeping bleep* until she can't tell her *bleepity bleep* from a gopher hole!''

Marie-Claire frowned. These sound effects made it difficult to keep up, but the gist of the matter was clear. Lula was upset with Ona.

Jerry arched a brow at the camera. "Let's bring out Ona.''

The audience hissed and jeered as the twenty-one-year-old Ona pranced out, looking three or four times her own age, but decidedly fighting the aging process kicking and screaming. Her leather bustier was two sizes too tight, squeezing her generous cleavage out the top.

And bottom.

Her nails were several inches long and festooned with racecars and tobacco slogans. Her wild hair was as brash as her makeup and her spiky heels had her towering over Lula. She shook her fist in a menacing fashion at the audience and then made a gesture to Lula that Marie-Claire figured had a more regional significance.

Nostrils flared, Lula lunged at Ona and Jerry smiled serenely at the camera. "Don't go away. We'll be right back with Junior, after these important messages."

Marie-Claire slowly nodded. Clearly, she needed to toughen up, if she was going to fight for her man. Perhaps she should practice her pithy expletives as well. A Tae-Bo class wouldn't hurt either, if Lula's high-kickin' style meant anything. And definitely she needed to reexamine her choices in clothing. She considered her wardrobe and realized she was far too conservative. Marie-Claire furiously scribbled some notes on her pad. Get in shape. Outrageous clothes.

Okay. Tongue protruding, she flipped through the channels till she landed on *The Ricki Lake Show*.

"Ricki, we used to think that men were from Mars and women were from Venus." The guest author gave her head a smug little wobble. "Wrong."

"Wrong?" Ricki leaned forward and frowned.

"Yes. We now know that men are really from Uranus."

"You're kidding."

"I know, it sounds far-fetched, but the key to success in a relationship with any man is knowing that *Real Men Are From Uranus*." The expert held up her new book and smiled.

Marie-Claire stuffed a handful of popcorn into her mouth. Uranus? Which one was that? She should have paid more attention in astronomy, she decided as she scribbled, find copy of *Real Men Are From Uranus* in palace library.

Pointing the remote, she next landed on *The Sally-Jesse Raphael Show*.

"Marsha," Sally-Jesse adjusted her signature glasses, "you realize that by not telling your son that he was adopted until he was a teenager, you were risking alienating him emotionally?"

"Sally, there just didn't seem to be any reason."

"Yes, but Marsha, clearly you and your husband are Caucasian. Chuck is African-American. Surely, you knew that someone would eventually let the cat out of the bag."

Marie-Claire scribbled, lies about adoption lead to alienation and again pointed the remote to pause at CNN.

"And in other international news, government officials in Rhineland today announced that they are making plans to reabsorb St. Michel, a tiny province just north of France. The two countries have existed independently from one another since the seventeenth century. A crucial water route leading from inland ports to the North Sea has been the subject of contention for years, more so now that St. Michel has recently upped the usage tax. In a statement made earlier today, St. Michel's Prime Minister Rene Davoine revealed that he has not met with Rhineland's Prince Etienne Kroninberg on this matter and has no immediate plans to do so. In other news..."

Marie-Claire snapped off the TV, feeling that she'd reached saturation with this venue and picked up a magazine. She peered at the cover she held. Why, in no time at all, according to this, she'd be ten pounds lighter and have her man eating out of her hand.

A sudden and loud pounding woke Marie-Claire with a start. Confused, she peeled her face from the shiny cover of the magazine upon which she'd been napping and blinked at her door.

"Marie-Claire?"

Sebastian! Flustered, she rolled over, rubbed her eyes and pushed her hair out of her face. A glance into the bottom of a full-length wall mirror told her everything she needed to know. Bad hair. Bad face. Bad mood.

Bad timing.

"Uh, who is it?" She hoped she sounded breezy. Cool.

Indifferent. Not as if she'd just been snoring and drooling on the cover of *Glamour*.

"It's me, Sebastian."

"Who?" Like a dog chasing its tail, Marie-Claire crawled in tight circles and wondered what to do first. What on earth was he doing here? He couldn't be here. She wasn't ready. She hadn't done all of her homework. Her order from Victoria's Secret had yet to arrive. And she still hadn't gotten through to Dr. Laura.

Okay, think.

She had to change her clothes. What would Ona wear? Certainly not the flouncy pink baby dolls that she sported now. No, Ona would wear something tight. Something made of leather and sheet metal screws. And she'd carry a whip.

"C'mon, Marie-Claire. Open up."

Up on her haunches, she gave her cheeks a couple of bracing smacks and glanced around the room. It looked as if a rebel faction bent on mass destruction had visited; self-help materials, books on adoption and genealogy and half-tested beauty products littered every spare area.

He could not come in here. No way.

Hands forming a plow, she shoved the mountain of magazines she'd been highlighting under her bed. Then, breathing hard, she clutched her comforter and attempted to haul herself to her feet. Unfortunately, the comforter came undocked and Marie-Claire fell back, pulling the great, downy monster over her head, where she grappled about, searching for terra firma. All nature of library books slid to the floor, along with some spicy lingerie catalogs and a volume on the history of the polygraph test.

"Marie-Claire, may I come in?"

Marie-Claire froze. Was that her door opening? He sounded awfully near.

The door closed and the sound of Sebastian's footsteps came from inside the room.

Chapter Eight

Rats. This was *not* the picture of sophistication she'd planned on exuding the next time she and Sebastian met. Static electricity had her hair standing on end as Marie-Claire peeked out from under the comforter. His shoes came into view first and she noted with chagrin that he was standing on a book whose title blared, *Combat Love*.

Her gaze traveled up his powerful legs, over his barrel chest and to his face. She saw thankfully that he was looking at her and not the book. Blood rushed up her neck and flooded her cheeks. Her heart pounded and she began to sweat.

She couldn't let him see that idiotic book.

"What are you doing?" he asked.

Her mind raced back to the vast sea of information and advice she'd collected over the last hours and came to a screeching halt at Ariane's pearl of wisdom. *Treat him like a brother. Isn't that what he wants? Do all the things a kid sister would do with a big brother.*

With a defiant toss of her head, she stared up at him,

nostrils flaring. ''Me? Well, since you're here, I was hoping we might, uh,'' she cast a panicky glance at the book beneath his feet, ''wrestle.''

She bit back a mortified groan.

Could she *be* any more idiotic? Her eyes slid closed at the image of her and Sebastian going for it, right there in the middle of her room, thumping and hollering and whatever it was kid brothers and sisters did when they were horsing around.

He gave his temple a quizzical scratch. ''Wrestle?''

''Sure.'' She could tell he thought she was nuts. Oh well, better nuts than a sobbing jilted lily, she guessed. ''Like this.'' Charging at him, headfirst, she collided with his shins, knocking him off balance and giving herself a dilly of a headache in the process.

''*Owww.*'' Their protests harmonized. She was going to kill Ariane.

As he fell to his knees, Marie-Claire launched the incriminating *Combat Love* book into her closet with a move she'd learned in soccer camp, back when she really was eight.

He stared at her, the disbelief in his voice warring with irritation. ''Are you crazy?''

Yes. Crazy in love. With a grunt, Marie-Claire clutched him around the thighs and tugged him completely off balance. They rolled around on the floor, Sebastian with bewilderment and Marie-Claire with purpose. Feet frantically scrambling, she winged the lingerie catalogs, along with a copy of a wedding magazine under her bed with the rest. Sebastian caught an errant fist in the process.

''What the hell? Owww! Marie-Claire, dammit, what are you doing? I don't want to wrestle with you.''

''What's wrong, pretty boy? Afraid I'll win?'' Elbowing her way over the top of his chest, she flailed about until she could flip her extremely private journal and a well-padded

WonderBra beneath her armoire. In this rather enjoyable process of tidying up, she accidentally managed to knee him in the jaw. The sound of his teeth crashing together gave her a twinge of sympathy, but really, she hadn't invited him to come snooping.

"Ouch! Damn! Auughh!" One hand flew to his jaw, the other to her ankle. "I think I just broke a tooth!"

"If you are very good, maybe the tooth fairy will leave some money under your pillow tonight."

An ominous growl suddenly had Marie-Claire questioning Ariane's logic. Perhaps this kid-sister thing was the wrong tack. Before she could ponder the issue further, Sebastian yanked her by the leg and she found herself flipped onto her back and lying beneath his body. After some heavy breathing and a lot of struggle, he managed to pinion her wrists together over her head. Her flouncy pink baby doll had tangled around her waist in a most provocative manner.

"I don't think this is a legal wrestling move." Marie-Claire grunted, wriggling about, trying to escape just far enough to pull her pajamas back down where they belonged.

"Tough," he growled and locked his feet around hers. Noses just a thumb's-width apart, he stared at her, and Marie-Claire could feel his lungs laboring and his heart pounding in tandem with hers. Their breath mingled, and Marie-Claire felt a yearning envelop her, nearly rendering her unconscious.

"Marie-Claire, why are you doing this?"

Hoping and praying she appeared casual, she breezed, "Isn't this what brothers and sisters do? I'm just trying to feel my way into our new relationship." Eyes wide with innocence, she blinked up at him.

He dropped his head. "Marie-Claire, you are making this very hard for me."

"Oh, and it's a walk in the park for me."

"I didn't say that."

"No, but you expect me to shift gears from lover to sister in less than a day. I'm trying to work with you here," she lied.

Misery flashed behind his eyes, and, though she felt for him, she took this as a good sign. He was no more ready to accept her as a sister than she was to receive him as a brother. Steeling herself against the powerful urge to give the poor guy a break, she gritted her teeth and continued her course.

"We have years of wrestling and jumping on the bed and tickling to make up for. Personally, I think we should do it all. It might bond us as siblings."

Aggravation pulled his mouth into a more severe curve and his eyes narrowed to slits of fury. "I don't think getting anywhere near the bed would be such a good idea." The frustration and impatience with her goading was palpable.

Her breathing became thready. Shallow.

He shifted, bringing his body into contact with hers from ankle to fingertip and Marie-Claire suddenly stilled as she realized that she now had him exactly where she wanted him. Even so, it was a hollow victory.

Come on, she silently urged him. You know the truth. We are not related.

"Okay." She gave a little shrug and angling her head so that her lips nearly touched his, she whispered, "Forget wrestling. How about a pillow fight instead?"

"How about a spanking?"

"Fine. I'll get the spoon. You drop your drawers." All right, she had to admit the bratty sister routine had gone too far. She needed to extend an olive branch, but it was hard to come up with the words with him looking at her as though he'd like to throttle her and then kiss her senseless.

Their eyes locked and attraction grew until the air between them seemed to crackle and burn. Marie-Claire could see that he was battling a fascination he found taboo. Forbidden.

Abruptly, he rolled onto his side and sat up. "I have to get back to the meeting." Tossing the comforter aside, he gripped her bedpost, hauled himself to his feet and stalked across the room.

She knee-walked after him. "Sebastian, wait!"

Head falling back on his shoulders, he paused in her doorway.

"Can you do this?" She rolled her tongue into the shape of a taco shell.

He turned and stared. "Marie-Claire, I don't know what you are—"

"Just do it!" she shouted.

Sebastian heaved a sigh of disgust and stuck his tongue out. However, try as he might, it lay there like a pink potato.

Marie-Claire grinned excitedly. "You're not my brother!"

"What?"

"You can't roll your tongue."

"What the hell does that have to do with anything?"

"It proves you are not related to me." Marie-Claire leveled an accusatory finger at him and fairly vibrated with victory. "The ability to roll your tongue is inherited!"

Sebastian's gaze darted at the ceiling for an instant, and then settled back on her face. "From whom? Your mother or your father?"

Marie-Claire frowned. "What?"

"When you are ready to grow up, we'll talk." The heavy slam of the door reverberated for a full minute after he left.

So. Marie-Claire flagged. Ariane's plan hadn't worked as quickly as she'd hoped. But she had sensed a chink in his armor. It was simply a matter of finding it.

* * *

With a resounding crack, Sebastian's club made contact with the ball. He watched, head back, eyes slit, as the golf ball took flight against the deep azure sky. If nothing else, this new twist in his relationship with Marie-Claire was improving his game. Straight as a builder's plumb line, the tiny white missile arced down the fairway. He picked up his tee, loaded his club, shouldered his bag and headed after his ball.

Golfing alone had never been Sebastian's style, but the last thing he wanted this afternoon was company.

He needed to think.

Marie-Claire had launched a deliberate offensive strike against his moratorium on their romance. She was doing everything in her power to thwart his stalwart efforts to protect her. To protect herself. From him. From the press. And, if she thought he couldn't see through these half-baked efforts, she had another think coming.

He felt a slow grin begin in his gut and spread up into his face as he remembered her antics earlier that day. Man, she was nuts. And that was precisely why he loved her. He shook his head, thinking a lesser woman would be content to give up the fight. To wallow in self-pity.

But not Marie-Claire de Bergeron.

No, Marie-Claire would lasso her man and flip him to the ground in record rodeo time. He laughed out loud, loving her more for loving him so fiercely. As his feet carried him across the grass, he remembered the teenaged banshee he'd first seen diving headlong into the pond. Then and there he'd known that he needed a woman with her pluck as his life partner. He'd never be content with a milquetoast type who had no fire in her belly.

On the other hand, she was causing a bit of a fire in his own guts, for heartburn was becoming a way of life these days. The very reasons he loved her beyond rational thought were the reasons she was driving him mad. Marie-Claire was trying to make him see why they should weather this conflagration together. Yet, he knew from years of experience that to do so would only put them further under the scrutiny of the public eye.

For now, he had to make her see that they couldn't be together.

Yet Sebastian knew that Marie-Claire was not out of wacky schemes. He rubbed the grin on his lips with his fingertips. The idea challenged him. Excited him. Made him feel like a player in the great game of life.

He slowed, then stopped. Clanking, his bag fell from his shoulder to the grass. Five iron in hand, he rocketed off another beauty. Yes, if he was going to win at the game of life with Marie-Claire, he was going to have to stay alert.

That evening, still sequestered in her room, Marie-Claire continued to study, though she was a bleary-eyed, emotional wreck from her skirmish with Sebastian. Gathering her hair and pushing it over her shoulder, she cast a tired glance around at the mess on her bedspread. There was so much advice. And so much of it was conflicting. Beside her lay a stack of yellow pads, filled with notes she'd compiled. Last on her list of self-imposed homework assignments for today was searching the Internet for newspaper advice columns that dealt with situations like hers.

Her head ached as she shifted her gaze onto the screen of her laptop. When she'd finished she would call Sebastian, apologize profusely, and then set the second part of her plan into motion.

Mouse in hand, she clicked and scanned and finally came upon a letter to Dr. Martha. Marie-Claire knew she'd find solid answers to difficult questions in her famous column.

Dear Dr. Martha:

My boyfriend of six years has suddenly decided that we need a break. Martha, I don't want a break. I'm desperately in love with him and hoping that someday soon, we'll marry. I know he loves me too, but something has him spooked. Any advice? I'll do whatever you say as I'm at my wit's end.

Signed,
Heartbroken in Hoboken

Empathy welled in Marie-Claire's throat as she plucked the last tissues from her second box of the day.

"Oh, Hoboken," she murmured into the screen of her laptop. "I know exactly how you feel." She scanned Dr. Martha's answer and realized that the general consensus from most experts seemed to come from the old adage: If you love someone, let him go. If it was meant to be, he will come back to you. If not, you're better off without him.

Better off without Sebastian?

No, she wouldn't be better off without him, but she'd never know if he was truly hers until she let go.

Or, at least until she gave the appearance of letting go.

She reached for the phone and punched in Sebastian's cell number. If she was going to apologize and then set him free, she had to do it now, before she lost her nerve. Waiting just one more minute would thwart all of her hard work and have her groveling at his stoop before sundown, begging him to come back the Lula Parnell way. And that was hardly attractive. Why did life have to be so bloody hard? She was a princess, for heaven's sake. Shouldn't she be living happily ever after just about now?

He picked up on the first ring.

"Sebastian?"

"Marie-Claire?" He sounded tentative. And thrilled. Tentatively thrilled, she guessed. Like her.

"Yes." The word sounded gushy. She cleared her throat. She closed her eyes. She needed to sound emotionally in control. A powerful woman, in charge of her destiny.

With her free hand, she clutched her teddy bear.

"The, uh, reason I'm calling is…" Why exactly was she calling? Oh, yes. To set him free. But then, hadn't he already taken care of that by setting himself free? Oh, this was so confusing. If one set oneself free, would one eventually come back?

"Marie-Claire?"

"I'm here. Sorry, I uh… Okay. I…I've had some time to think it over and I just wanted to tell you, that I think you're right."

"Right?"

"Yes. Absolutely right."

There was a silence on his end.

"Sebastian?"

"Yes, I'm…here."

"Oh. Good. Now then. I also wanted to apologize for my idiotic behavior this afternoon, and to beg your forgiveness. After all, if you are going to be my," the bile rose at the very word, "brother, we will be seeing a lot of each other, around the house, at parties, at our…" she choked, then continued with strangled gaiety, "respective weddings and such."

"Marie-Claire, if you would just—"

"No, no, no. Please. Just let me finish. I wanted to let you know, that it's taken some time, but I've come around to the idea that we are…uh…siblings…and I embrace it. Really. In the most mature sense of our…relationship. For Papa's sake. For your sake."

For heaven's sake, she thought, feeling the panic rise. This had sure as hell better work.

"So," she continued brightly, "I promise to make you proud. You don't have to worry about me...er...fawning after you anymore—"

"I don't?"

"No, no," Marie-Claire hastened to assure. "I realize that none of this is our fault. We couldn't have known. And, so, the best thing would be to...to...to...carry on as if nothing had ever happened."

"Nothing? Marie-Claire, for pity sa—"

"Right. To become just one big, happy family. It's for the best. And...and...and...I think that we should—" again, a surge of stomach bile threatened to choke her. She took a cleansing breath and was glad she was lying down. "—I think that we should begin dating other people as soon as possible. For appearances' sake, wouldn't you agree?"

"For...appearances' sake?"

"I'm sure it's the only way. For me, anyway. I need to get you out of my system. Now. And the best way I can think of would be to move on."

Silence.

"Sebastian?"

"You want to move on?"

"Yes."

"So soon?"

"I must. I can't take this stress anymore. It's not like I can sit around and wait for the opportunity to marry my own brother, now, can I?"

"You know damn good and well that's not what I want—"

"That's...that's wonderful. In that case, you won't mind if I bring a date upon occasion to the dinner table. For the sake of appearances, of course."

He snorted. "Of course."

"And, to further my emotional healing, I thought I might start by inviting a date to accompany me to the press conference party tomorrow night."

"Marie-Claire, you do what you have to do."

Was that the tiniest trace of a smirk in his voice? Did he think she was bluffing? Well, she most certainly wasn't. Irked at his arrogance, she said, "Okay. I will."

"You do that."

"Fine."

"Fine."

"Good-bye."

"Good-bye." Marie-Claire hung up then slapped her forehead so hard she saw stars. Oh, great. Now she had to come up with a date. A quick glance at the clock told her that she had less than twenty-four hours to achieve that particular lunacy.

"I don't know why they didn't announce *you* as crown prince during that ridiculous excuse for a press conference today." Expression sour, Claudette fussed at her reflection in a giant gilt-framed mirror that hung just outside the Sapphire Salon in the de Bergeron Palace. It took a number of amazing facial gyrations to get her lipstick and mascara just so, while Sebastian stood impatiently by. "All this inane chatter about Rhineland plotting against us," she muttered, "when we know the only story worth telling is the fact that my son will soon be king!"

Myriad cosmetics were snapped shut and tossed into her bag and with a flutter of her lashes, Claudette declared herself ready. Not wanting to give her time to linger before the mirror, Sebastian took her arm and led her into the crowd that streamed toward the Celebration of Independence Gala that was to begin momentarily in the Crystal Ballroom.

For the last hour, Claudette and Sebastian had been honored guests at the Saturday afternoon press conference, sharing box seats with the royal family in the spacious auditorium designed for just such events. Prime Minister Rene Davoine spoke at length about plans to negotiate with Rhineland to circumvent a crisis situation between the two countries over water rights.

Embarrassingly, Claudette had nodded off during part of the speech and even managed to time her snores during the dramatic pauses. The titters of the audience had jolted her awake and she'd laughed with the crowd about a joke that was upon herself.

And that was only the beginning of this miserable night, Sebastian feared. This was a "game face" party, designed to prove to Rhineland that they were not quaking in their boots about the threats being handed down. Though Sebastian was not attending in an official capacity, he knew he was being "test-driven" by Simone. She wanted to see if he had what it took to be king someday.

Although, according to the laws that made this a male monarchy, if he was indeed Philippe's son, he already had the stuff it took.

Stomach churning, Sebastian continued his grip on Claudette's arm and marched stoically toward what would no doubt be one of the most trying nights of his life. That Claudette had been invited to attend had his head throbbing and his eye twitching. But the knowledge that Marie-Claire would be there, with a date no less, made him want to beat up one of the statues standing poised for battle in the gargantuan hall.

Puffing to keep pace with Sebastian's lengthy stride, Claudette was still clucking like the snubbed hen. "A word from Simone, introducing you to the world, wouldn't have killed her. In fact, it would have put Rhineland and its king, that disgusting, impotent Giraud Kroninberg in his proper place, if that's what they really wanted to do. I don't know what they're waiting for."

Sebastian turned down a deserted side hall and swung on Claudette. Hand-to-wall, nose-to-nose, he hovered over her. "They are waiting to find out if your version of history is true."

Claudette gaped at him, expression wounded. "Why would they even question my word?"

"You tell me."

"I will not! Don't be ridiculous. St. Michel is in desperate need of a king and you are the man for the job. Who better suited than you?"

"No one," Sebastian hissed and raked his hands through his hair as he checked around for the ever-curious paparazzi, "—*if* I was born to the job. But you'll have to forgive me, Mère, if I'm a little reticent about taking the position. I have never aspired to be the crown prince of this country, let alone king. I still have no desire whatsoever to fill Philippe's shoes. Especially since you waited until the eleventh hour to tell anyone the supposed truth."

"What are you *saying?*" Claudette asked, horror-stricken. "You would pass up a once-in-a-lifetime opportunity because you don't *feel* like taking the job? I have moved heaven and earth to get you to the point you are today and you are going to throw it all away? I'll not have it!"

"*You'll* not have it?"

"You will take your rightful spot! With a simple nod of acceptance we could be set for life. Do you have any idea what that means? *Do you?*" Her shrill voice caused several heads from the crowd in the main hallway to dip in and look.

Skin crawling, Sebastian stared at his mother. Elevated

blood pressure encouraged beads of sweat on Claudette's brow and, as he stood motionless watching her rant, the suspicion that had begun as a tiny seed of doubt began to take root. Something about the urgency on her part was eerie. A peculiar light would gleam in her eye whenever she talked about him being Philippe's son, and it was almost as if she'd managed to convince herself it was true.

Whether or not it was.

"Mère," he gritted out through a tight jaw, "this is neither the time nor the place for such a conversation. I'll take you home and we can finish this discussion there."

"Are you out of your mind? And miss the Gala Ball?" Her eyes bulged at the very thought. "Never!" With that, chin high, fancy heels a-tapping, Claudette whirled around and stormed off to join the party in progress.

Just one flight up, Marie-Claire stared at the booty spread out across her bed in hapless fascination. She picked up what looked like a punch bowl festooned with faux fruit and wads of sparkly netting and settled it at a rakish angle on her head. What on earth had she been thinking, bidding on this uncertain fashion statement? Must have been swept up in the moment. Her purse, with its tropical birds and authentic "rain forest palm frond weave" was no tamer.

That morning, with her sisters at her side, Marie-Claire had enjoyed front-row seats at a catwalk fashion show for charity in Paris. The spring collection featured haute couture from Milan, London and New York and—she fingered her gaudy new hat—Uranus.

In the full-length mirror across the room she studied the strange apparition that was her reflection. Was she trying to attract Sebastian or scare him to death? The gold lamé dress she wore could surely be detected by radar and, like the ones on Ona Parnell's feet, the pointy, super high-heeled boots could put an eye out. Her new hair, makeup and nail styles also had a space-age quality, all spiky and metallic and—she was assured by her sisters—sexy.

Marie-Claire worried her glittery lower lip with her teeth. She'd made the mistake of telling her sisters she wanted to look a little naughty. Decadent.

Wicked.

In the nicest possible sense of the word, of course. Well, they'd taken the ball and run, and now, Marie-Claire turned and glanced over her shoulder to inspect her backside, she feared Cruella De Vil would look like a nun in comparison. Never mind. Her gaze traveled back to her bed. Surely something from this pile of spare auto parts that passed for the world of fashion's finest would make Sebastian sit up and realize that she was no sister of his.

Anxiously, she fingered the sleeve of a faux zebra coat.

But what if he didn't?

Suddenly depressed, Marie-Claire sagged to the edge of her mattress. She absolutely hated everything she'd bought, and couldn't imagine anyone in their right mind going out in public in any of this stuff. She wanted her old life back. A tear slowly rolled down her cheek. She wanted her Papa back. Her legitimacy back. Her boyfriend back.

With a bang, her bedroom door burst open. Wearing their own purchases from today's Parisian fashion extravaganza, Lise and Ariane swept into her room, full of life and ready to party. She swiped at her tears with her pinky fingers and forced herself to smile. Ariane looked fetching in her micro-mini and peacock feather vest and Lise was all the modern mommy in a tummy-hugging tube gown that had her taking tiny, shuffling steps.

Yes. It took guts to pull off a bold fashion statement, Marie-Claire decided. More guts than she had. Though, she had to admit that her sisters did look chic in a garish, avant-garde sort of way.

"Marie-Claire! You look fabulous!" they gushed when they saw her hunched at the edge of her bed.

"Doesn't she look fabulous?"

"Fabulous."

Marie-Claire harrumphed. "I look like a satellite dish with cleavage."

"No! You're perfect! Isn't she perfect, Lise?"

"Perfect."

"You don't think the hat is too much?"

Lise gave her head an emphatic shake. "No! All that's coming back into vogue, you know."

"No." Heaven forbid. Marie-Claire fingered her crazy headdress. Her neck was killing her and the night had only just begun.

"I have a date all sewn up for you," Ariane announced as she made herself at home at Marie-Claire's vanity and began applying a coat of silver lipstick. "He's not perfect, but on such short notice, it was the best I could do."

"What's wrong with him?

"Well, he's a little young."

"How young?"

"He's not jailbait, if that's what you're afraid of."

Marie-Claire dropped her face into her hands and moaned. "What have you done? Who is this…date?"

"Why worry yourself unnecessarily about who he is? Let it be a surprise. In the meantime, spritz your hair with that glitter spray you paid a fortune for today. We've got a party to attend."

Chapter Nine

The Crystal Ballroom had become an undulating mass of humanity. From where she stood with her sisters at the top of the stairs, Marie-Claire could see a popular British rock band up high on the main stage, their throbbing bass beat underscoring the din of conversation and laughter. Colored spotlights hit the giant Austrian-crystal chandeliers, scattering tiny rainbow prisms like fireflies over the band and revelers.

The party, open to the public at a minimal cost, was designed as a continental nose-thumbing at Rhineland. To show solidarity and independence, as it were, among the people of St. Michel. That being the case, security guards were roaming in abundance. Everywhere, the St. Michel flag was proudly displayed, and the festive décor reflected the country's colors of gold, white and royal purple.

This would be a night to remember.

Hand to banister, Marie-Claire clutched the highly polished wood and attempted to slow her breathing and gather her nerve. Sebastian was somewhere in this room. Like the princess who knew there was a pea under her stack of mattresses, she could feel him in the crowd. Trying to appear blasé, she allowed her gaze to drift like a feather on a light breeze.

"Celeste is here," Lise said, lifting her voice to be heard above the ruckus and, leaning toward Marie-Claire, pointed out their stepmother.

"Mmm."

"Gauging from her outfit, it would seem she is tired of mourning already." Ariane snorted. "She is dressed more ridiculously than we are. What on earth is she trying to prove?"

"And who is that she's flirting with?" Lise squinted over Ariane's shoulder.

"He is paparazzi."

"Oh, great." Sighing heavily, Marie-Claire covered her face with her hands and groaned. "Could my life get any weirder?"

"Is that Luc Dumont?" Ariane leaned back and pointed to another corner of the room. All three heads swung to see.

"Where?"

"Over there…see the woman in that garish, multicolored, retro caftan? Behind her."

Marie-Claire looked in the direction Ariane's finger pointed. "The woman in the garish caftan is Claudette LeMarc."

Sure enough, the ebullient Claudette snagged a drink from a passing tray and seemed unaware that she was the object of such intense scrutiny as she tapped her feet and snapped her fingers to the beat of the music. She was obviously having a ball, surrounded by socialite girlfriends, equally snooty. And equally inebriated.

"And, yes," Marie-Claire said and frowned, "the guy

behind her is Luc. I wonder what he's doing here? I thought Simone let him go?''

''From the way he is staring, I think maybe he has a hankering for Claudette.'' Ariane and Lise giggled.

Marie-Claire relaxed enough to allow herself a smile until she noticed who was standing not five paces from Claudette.

Sebastian.

As if she were dangling from a cliff, her vital functions seemed to suspend with the emotions—supposedly forbidden—that coursed through her. Desire, fright and excitement all warred within for dominance.

He seemed to feel her gaze the second she spotted him. Their eyes met in a collision so jarring, the controlled mayhem faded away and they became the only two people in the room. Head tilted back, Sebastian's thickly lashed eyes were at half mast, slowly perusing her from head to toe and finally settling on her face. His expression betrayed his less-than-brotherly interest. Her bashful gaze dipped and rose again only to have her smile flash-freeze and her rapidly pumping heart crash into her stomach, a leaden, lifeless lump.

Veronike.

How had she failed to notice Veronike Schroeder plastered to his side like a blond body cast? Jealousy sliced through Marie-Claire as she watched Veronike whisper something to Sebastian and then laugh her throaty, husky, steamy-hot, wide-mouthed, disgusting laugh.

''She laughs like a braying donkey.'' Ariane sniffed, and threw a sisterly arm around Marie-Claire's waist. Lise squeezed her shoulder. ''And in that plunging neckline, she looks like a dairy cow.''

Marie-Claire shot them tremulous smiles of gratitude, even as her heart was dissolving. She blinked back the tears.

"Belly-breathe, Marie-Claire," Ariane advised. "You're looking a little pale."

"Don't let Veronike get your goat, honey. She's not worth getting upset over."

Like the managers of a prize fighter, Lise and Ariane rubbed her arms and patted her back and spoke words meant to encourage. Glassy-eyed, Marie-Claire soaked it all in and knew that she had to listen or run. And Marie-Claire never ran.

Her sisters were right. She wasn't going to let some braying bovine get the better of her. She was a de Bergeron! Anger sluiced through her, roiling in her gut, routing out the fear.

"Now, laugh, Marie-Claire. Show them what you're made of."

Obediently, Marie-Claire opened her mouth wide and, shoulders bobbing, hooted.

"Is she laughing or crying?" Lise wondered.

"Can't tell." Ariane peered into Marie-Claire's face. "Are you all right, Marie-Claire?"

"Fine," Marie-Claire gritted and swiped at the tears that swam in her eyes. *So.* It seemed that whatever remorse Sebastian had felt over losing her was short-lived. Well. She clamped her mouth shut. If he could recover from undying love overnight, she guessed she could, too. Sebastian LeMarc would soon see that she did not need him to have a good time. She did not need him to go on living. Breathing.

Standing.

Marie-Claire clutched at Ariane's arm with both hands and, inhaling deeply through her nose, squared her shoulders. She, too, had a date. Somewhere.

"Ariane?" she chirped. "My date?"

"Oh. Ahhh, yes. Your...date."

She followed Ariane's guilty gaze down the long stair to…Eduardo Van Groober.

Marie-Claire's momentary burst of confidence took a direct hit.

"Eduardo?" she asked dully.

"Should I have warned you?"

"You should have shot me."

"Smile," Ariane said, "everyone is looking."

Indeed, everyone was looking. Paparazzi flashes strobed and Marie-Claire was momentarily blinded.

Fumbling, bumbling, stumbling, Eduardo took the stairs three at a time, a mangled corsage in one hand, and a pearl-headed corsage pin in the other. "Oh, Marie-Claire. You look, you look, you're…*très chic!*" When he reached her, he was breathing hard and reeling with zeal. "I brought you a corsage. Here, I can…pin…somewhere…just…"

Unprepared for his effusive welcome, Marie-Claire—still blinded and teetering on Ona-style shoes—was thrown off balance when the tip of Eduardo's three-inch pin found the soft flesh above her breast. Surprised by the stabbing pain, Marie-Claire's ankles collapsed and she rode the sides of her feet down several steps before she managed to grasp the railing.

Ariane and Eduardo rushed after her, while at the same time a concerned Lise hippity-hopped about in her tube dress, trying to catch an avalanche of faux grapes and bananas before they escaped.

Fortunately, it worked.

Unfortunately, a heel had snapped off one of her fancy butt-kickin' shoes.

Fortunately, she never planned on wearing this garish outfit again.

Unfortunately, her rather skimpy gold lamé dress had ridden up her thighs and her hat was now on backwards.

Fortunately, Marie-Claire no longer cared if she lived or died.

Sebastian's heart lurched into his throat as he watched Marie-Claire stumble and then right herself. He took a step forward, but a surge of men beat him to the punch and he could see that she already had plenty of eager assistance. Frustrated beyond belief, he ran a hand over his jaw and around to the stiff muscles at the back of his neck.

Tonight, Marie-Claire was more beautiful than ever before. Her leggy figure was enveloped in some kind of form-fitting, shiny gold dress that accentuated her perfect curves and had every man in the room drooling. Her long, shapely legs appeared even longer in those wild, metallic boots and her hair and makeup were amazing. Trendy. Space-age. Beautiful. She looked like something straight off a Paris catwalk, and Veronike, though she pretended disdain, knew it.

Beads of sweat broke out on his brow and his Adam's apple worked against his bow tie. Searing jealousy, not only of Eduardo, but of every man in the damned room who was fawning over Marie-Claire and helping her right her hat and dress and…fruit, clawed at his heart.

Out of the benevolent bedlam that swirled around him, came a deeply melancholy moment.

How the hell had it come to this? Mere weeks ago, they were the happy couple. And now, here he stood, holding up the limp and clinging Veronike, and Marie-Claire was dating the Van Groober boy.

Certainly, Eduardo was more her own age, but really, was she *interested* in him? It sure looked like it, by the way she was fawning over the corsage he'd just pinned to her breast.

"The children seem to be enjoying themselves," Veronike murmured, gesturing to the stairs. "It looks as if little

Marie-Claire has finally got herself a boyfriend. He's cute. He seems to make her very happy.''

Sebastian had to admit it looked as if she was right. Head thrown back, Marie-Claire was laughing gaily at something witty Eduardo had just said.

"Marie-Claire, I'm so sorry. You're…you're bleeding there.''

Sucking her breath between her teeth, Marie-Claire's head fell back and she winced at the ceiling. She tried to swallow her groans of pain and reassure him, but the pin had plunged deep into the muscle, and it hurt like the dickens. She wondered when she'd had her last tetanus booster. She forced herself to emit some strangled laughter in order to spare his feelings. "It'll be all right, Eduardo.''

"Oh, good." Relief flooded his face, causing his freckles to blend back into his usually ruddy complexion. "Would you care to dance?''

"Uh, well, Eduardo, actually, I'd like to make it down the stairs in one piece first, and then we'll see, all right?''

"Right! Allow me." He held out his arm and miraculously, they descended the stair without further mishap. "One time, I was working with my dad out in the palace garden, when I was a little kid and I stepped on this nail—''

"Isn't that nice?'' On autopilot, Marie-Claire smiled and nodded, mentally measuring the distance between her and Sebastian.

"—and I had to go to the hospital and have surgery, because it tore up a bunch of ligaments—''

"That's great!'' He was not five meters away. And, he was watching her. Marie-Claire felt her stomach turn to liquid.

"—thought I'd never walk again, but I did! But the only sport I could play was golf—''

Marie-Claire stared past Sebastian as if he wasn't there, even though she mentally documented and categorized every breath he took.

"—because I was so clumsy and so she was really scared after I broke my leg in our school's production of *Les Mis*—"

"That must have been fun." Marie-Claire managed to trump up some more happy-go-lucky laughter and feared that her face would crack with the continual effort. And, though she stared at Eduardo as if his conversation was riveting, she never lost track of Sebastian's whereabouts.

Even across the room, she could feel the raw sexuality Sebastian exuded. Every woman could, it seemed. Even Grandmama Simone, who was currently pestering him for a dance. The gentle way he took the elderly woman into his arms had Marie-Claire smiling in spite of herself. The fact that he was dancing with a queen seemed not to faze him, the way it would have other men in the room. The old girl suddenly looked sixty years younger in his arms.

When the song had ended, Sebastian returned Simone to the sidelines and thanked her for the dance. The entire time they had moved about the floor, he could tell he was being scrutinized. Dissected. It seemed to him Simone thought that if by staring hard enough, she could see the shadow of her Philippe in his expression. She seemed blue and it occurred to Sebastian that on a night not at all unlike this, Simone had lost her only son.

With a squeeze of her knobby hands, he kissed the powdery-soft, paper-thin flesh of her cheek and whispered, "Adieu."

Her smile was half-hearted as she whispered back, "Adieu," with a ring of finality that had him wondering what exactly she knew in her heart.

Alone at last, Sebastian turned his attentions to spotting Marie-Claire. He found her with Eduardo who was asserting his manhood by seizing Marie-Claire and pressing her to his scrawny chest. In a clench that nearly lifted her feet from the floor, he steered her through the crowd, his ill-defined style all jerks and stops like a dog with a rag doll. A lesser woman would have cried whiplash and begged off. Yet, Marie-Claire managed to extricate herself from his clutches and make him look like a halfway decent partner.

Ignoring Eduardo, no doubt out of self-preservation more than anything, Marie-Claire's eyes fell closed and her hips swayed. Sebastian felt his chest tighten. She was a wonderful dancer, seeming to feel the music and letting it flow through her body.

With a groan, Sebastian flexed his hands and fought his never-ending reactions to her. Would it be like this for the rest of his life? If she were indeed his sister, every moment they spent in the same room together would be sheer hell. There was no way on God's green earth that he was going to be able to live like this, wanting something just out of his grasp but never having satisfaction.

If Claudette was telling the truth, there was only one way this thing could go. One of them would have to leave St. Michel.

Forever.

Exhausted from what seemed like an eon of being dragged around the dance floor by the sweaty Eduardo, Marie-Claire beseeched him to find her a cup of punch. Thirsty himself, Eduardo trotted in search of beverages, while Marie-Claire found a vacant chair off in a corner alone. Wearily, she sat, feeling the ache of every bone in her body. Making Sebastian notice what a wonderful time she was having without him was hideous work. Especially in a pair of boots that sported only one heel.

While she waited for Eduardo to bring her a cup of punch, she scanned the room for Sebastian and, unfortunately, found him, dancing once again with Veronike. Morbid fascination held Marie-Claire in its grip and she watched Veronike provocatively thrust her pelvis in time to the music. Like a cat in heat, she strutted in tight circles around Sebastian, rubbing her voluptuous body up against his and smiling a half-awake Marilyn Monroe-type smile. Marie-Claire could practically hear her purr.

In comparison to the flashy, experienced Veronike, Marie-Claire felt like a clunker limping along on a flat tire.

Luc Dumont moved to stand next to Marie-Claire and indicated Veronike with a nod of his head. "I never did learn how to dance."

"That is not dancing. That's the mating ritual of the socially challenged."

"Ah. Looks as if it's working."

"Yes, it does, doesn't it?" Marie-Claire sighed. "We haven't been formally introduced. You are Luc?"

Luc held out his hand. "Dumont. Yes. Forgive my breach of etiquette."

"Of course. I'm Marie-Claire de Bergeron."

"Yes. I'm pretty familiar with everyone in your family."

"So you are. I noticed that you are acquainted with Juliet."

"We met some years ago, yes. She's lovely."

"She is indeed. So. Tell me, Mr. Dumont," Marie-Claire tore her gaze from Sebastian and Veronike long enough to dart him a curious smile, "why are you still hanging around? I thought the case of the missing heir had been solved."

Luc shrugged. "Maybe."

Marie-Claire's brows flew up. "Maybe not?"

"Maybe."

At that moment, Claudette danced by with the prime minister and, with a covert look about to see who was watching, steered poor Mr. Davoine into the path of the paparazzi. Bulbs flashed. Claudette's smile was triumphant. By morning their picture would be splashed across the society pages.

Knowing intrinsically that she could trust him, Marie-Claire decided to confide her fears about Claudette in Luc.

"I think she is lying."

"You, too?"

"So we agree."

"I believe I could unearth enough dirt to fill several books."

"Really?" Marie-Claire patted the chair next to her and when Luc was seated, she leaned toward him. "What do *you* think Claudette's motivation for lying could be? Everyone knows that she's a social climber, but to sacrifice her son? To chance being discovered? To what end?"

"Desperation. From what I've been able to find out, she is in debt up to her diamond earrings. I believe she has her sights set on the royal payroll."

"Really," Marie-Claire murmured, feeling almost sorry for the woman. Claudette had no idea what a treasure she already had in Sebastian. "What do you suggest we do?"

"Tonight? Nothing."

"Nothing?"

"Without the proper proof, there is nothing we can do. But don't fret. Time is on our side."

As Marie-Claire watched Veronike ooze to the beat around Sebastian, Eduardo, cups of punch sloshing, stumbled in her direction. She sighed.

"Mr. Dumont, I'm running out of time."

* * *

Marie-Claire needed air.

Looking a little flushed himself, Eduardo was only too happy to accompany her out of doors. She could feel Sebastian's eyes watching as they swept by, Eduardo chattering about the computer club and chess team, and she limping along and pretending to hang on his every word.

When they got out to the verandah, Eduardo dropped a casual arm around her shoulders. At first, Marie-Claire enjoyed the rather romantic gesture thinking, let Sebastian stick this in his pipe and smoke it.

Then Eduardo grinned at her, and a chill ran down her spine at the quixotic expression on his face. The way his teeth protruded between his lips, gleaming in the moonlight, suddenly struck Marie-Claire as somewhat feral. Vampirish. That, coupled with the fact that his hand had just slid to her bottom, had her wondering exactly what was in that punch he'd been guzzling for the last half hour.

"I can't believe we are finally here, together," he husked, "alone."

Marie-Claire emitted some uncomfortable laughter and pointed out, "Not completely alone. There are several thousand people right back there, in the ballroom."

Eduardo ignored that fact and, nostrils flaring, buried his face in her hair and inhaled. "I've been dreaming of this moment ever since I was in the seventh grade and I saw you ride out to the pond for a swim." He blew several strands of her hair out of his mouth, scratched his face and went back to snuffling. "You were so beautiful. I was going to tell you that I was there, fishing on the other side of the pond, but Sebastian came and told you to get out of the water."

"You...were *there*?"

"Don't worry. I didn't see everything." He chuckled and

his other hand slipped to join the first one at her bottom. "I think that's where I fell in love with you."

"In—" Marie-Claire swallowed, "—*love?*"

"Yes, I have a scrapbook filled with pictures of you."

Uh-oh. A lump of foreboding rose into her throat. Reaching behind her, she gripped his wrists, attempting to keep his boa-constrictor act in check. "Uh, Eduardo? I think we should go back—"

"Marie-Claire," Eduardo rooted around at the side of her neck, "I know that we were meant to be together. I've known it ever since that night."

"Y-Y-You have?"

"Yes." Teeth leading, he traversed her jaw and headed for her mouth.

"Oh, Eduardo." Flabbergasted, Marie-Claire strained back, chin to neck, leaning as far away as his steely grip would allow. She tried to act as if she knew he was teasing. "This is our first date. You can't be in love with me."

As she uttered the words, she knew that wasn't exactly accurate. That same night at the pond was enough time to press Sebastian into her heart for time and eternity. Marie-Claire was losing the battle as Eduardo slowly forced her forward for a little kiss. The confidence in her voice turned to pleading.

"Oh, no, no thank you, Eduardo."

"Just one kiss, Marie-Claire. Then you'll see."

"No, Eduardo, I don't think that would be such a goo—"

Eduardo's lips crashed down on hers and Marie-Claire feared she was bleeding from the collision.

"Mmm….eee…Eduar-dooo, no, please don't. I said…no, Eduardo." Frantically, Marie-Claire squirmed, trying to pry his hands from around her waist, but Eduardo tightened his hold. His hands, incredibly strong now, roved from her hips to the top of her zipper and Marie-Claire feared he was going to disrobe her then and there.

Tears of humiliation welled in her eyes. Damn her foolish pride. She wouldn't be in this predicament if she hadn't been trying to torture Sebastian. Ashamed, she pushed against Eduardo until he suddenly popped away like a cork from a champagne bottle. Her eyes widened as she marveled at her strength.

Until she saw Sebastian.

Holding Eduardo by the scruff of his neck, Sebastian growled, "Eduardo, man, did you hear the woman? She said no. Snap out of it."

Fists flying in the air, Eduardo took a swing at Sebastian and managed to land a solid punch to his gut.

"*Owww!*"

A kick to the shins had Sebastian gasping with pain yet again.

"Dammit, Eduardo. Stop it, man. That *hurts!*"

"No!" Eduardo panted, still flailing. Though Sebastian held the boy at arm's length by the head, he was just lanky enough to do some pretty serious damage.

"*Don't hurt him, Sebastian,*" Marie-Claire screamed.

Sebastian turned to stare at her. "Do I...*ufff, dammit Eduardo*...do I *look* like I'm hurting him?"

"It's all my fault," she sobbed.

"Leave us alone," Eduardo shouted.

"No," Marie-Claire cried.

Sebastian dropped his head and gave it a disgusted shake. "Will you two make up your minds?"

"She wants me. She cares for me, I know it." Eduardo's protestations grew pathetic. "Tell him, Marie-Claire. Tell him how much we have in common...tell him."

"Oh, Eduardo. I'm so sorry." Marie-Claire sagged

against the concrete railing and pushed her hair out of her face. "I…I'm in love with someone else."

Sebastian's eyes fell closed.

Her words had a sobering effect on Eduardo as well and the boy flagged. His miserable smile was without rancor as he drew himself up and stepped away from Sebastian. "I knew it was too good to be true."

As he ran a hand over his bruised belly, Sebastian said, "Eduardo, no woman likes to be pawed to death on the first date."

"You know—" Eduardo's laughter was mirthless as he dropped his head into his hands and moaned. "I'm such a jerk."

"No more so than I, Eduardo," Marie-Claire said. "I've made such a fool of myself tonight. I'm so sorry if I gave you the wrong impression."

"Don't be." He stood for a long, silent moment, then said, "Maybe tonight was one of those horrible experiences that we will look back on one day and laugh."

"I will if you will."

Eduardo smiled his boyish, buck-toothed smile, and Marie-Claire could see that someday he would grow into a decent man. "It's a date, then."

With a nod at her and then at Sebastian, Eduardo brushed himself off, straightened his cummerbund and shuffled back into the party.

Sebastian watched in silence as Marie-Claire dropped to a concrete bench beside the low row of fat balustrades. Gingerly, she removed her boots, then tossed them over the rail and into the bushes. The hat and fruit followed. With her thumbs, she began to rub circles into the soles of her feet, little mewling moans ushering forth from her throat. He longed to sit next to her and take her feet into his lap, and do that for her, but prudence allowed him to come only as far as the end of the bench.

"Sebastian." She didn't look up as she spoke, seeming more interested in her feet than in the message she began to impart without emotion. "I've been such an idiot. I've been letting other people tell me what to do as far as you are concerned, and that's been a terrible mistake."

The concrete was cold and rough against his palms as he backed up to the railing and stood, ankles crossed. "It hasn't been easy, Marie-Claire. For either of us."

"No. But I have to tell you that I can't go on like this. I will never be able to accept you as a brother. It's simply impossible. And, since you won't accept me as your love—"

"I can't right *now,* Marie-Claire! You know why!"

"Do I, Sebastian?" She stopped rubbing and looked up at him.

Hands flexing, Sebastian wrestled with his frustration. Even if Claudette was not telling the truth, the very hint of doubt hanging over their relationship would be devastating. Marie-Claire had no idea how damaging a rumor of incest would be. She thought she could handle the fallout, but until they had to face that particular disgrace, she couldn't begin to understand.

Marie-Claire dropped her feet to the ground and standing, padded to stand directly in front of him. Laying her cheek on his chest, she circled his waist with her slender arms and sighed a light sigh of homecoming. Her familiar scent enveloped him: soap and something floral in her hair and perfume and fresh air, all combined to produce a powerful aphrodisiac for him.

She tilted her face up to his. "I refuse to let other people run my life. Why don't you?"

Like a martyr on his way to slaughter, Sebastian wilted,

his eyes dropping shut. *Because I'm trying to protect you,* he wanted to shout. Instead, he said, "Because we can't always have what we want, when we want it."

"Not even when it's right?" Marie-Claire whispered, her lips a hairbreadth from his, the taboo quotient holding him motionless except for their labored breathing.

Never had he wanted to kiss anyone more than he wanted to kiss Marie-Claire at that moment. Never had he been more tortured. But, until there was conclusive evidence, the return of the DNA tests that Luc had covertly sent off to the lab in Chicago, there was no way he could chance her reputation. And, even though it was killing him, he could not even give Marie-Claire the slightest hint that she might be right. To do so would only invite disaster.

"Sebastian, I don't care what your mother says. I don't care what the world thinks. I love you. Shouldn't that be enough?"

"It should. But it's not."

"Sebastian, please."

Unable to take another second of this torment, Sebastian did the only thing he knew how. The only thing that could save her from herself. From scandal and public humiliation that would haunt her for the rest of her life.

He withdrew her hands from around his waist and stepped back. "Marie-Claire, stop it. We cannot be together. Not now. Maybe—maybe not ever." Though it was killing him, Sebastian turned and walked away without looking back to see her reaction.

For to do so would only have him running back to carry her off. And he loved her too much to do that.

Just inside, he found Veronike waiting for him. A sixth sense had her offering her mouth to his for a kiss and though he was loath to do so, he took her up on her offer, then led her to the dance floor.

Chapter Ten

Numb with grief, Marie-Claire couldn't even cry. For hours now, she'd been sitting by her window, staring at the twilight sky. Outside, the sounds of dawn reached her through an open window and the whisper of a cool breeze caressed her face. On the ground below, the servants who'd cleaned up after the gala were leaving for home. Voices murmured their partings, car engines rumbled to life. Off in the distance, a rooster heralded the advent of a new day and, at a table by her side a lone candle burned low, hissing.

Dully, Marie-Claire shifted her gaze to the flickering flame and saw her life.

It was over.

Even if Sebastian was not the crown prince, she knew that her foolishness had lost him forever to Veronike. Or, if not Veronike, some other woman who wouldn't go to such ridiculous lengths to prove her love.

She blinked once, then shifted her unseeing stare back out the window. Why would she and Sebastian harbor such intense feelings for each other for five long years only to have it come to such a disastrous end? It simply did not make sense.

A light tapping at her door interrupted her wretched ruminations. Ariane appeared, carrying a valise and dressed in a sensible wool traveling suit. Quite a change from the last time she'd entered the room, Marie-Claire reflected, lifting a hand in despondent greeting.

Ariane set her purse and bag on Marie-Claire's bed and then silently moved across the room. Gently, her fingers combed through Marie-Claire's hair and she whispered, "I just stopped by to tell you goodbye."

"Already?"

"It's Sunday morning."

Marie-Claire nodded. "So. You are off to Rhineland."

"Yes."

"Why?"

Ariane's chuckle rang false as she fussed with a small tangle of strands. "Why? Because Etienne invited me, of course."

"He *invited* you?" Marie-Claire briskly rubbed her face with her hands. Life just kept getting curiouser and curiouser, as Alice would have said when confronted with Wonderland. "Ariane, in the past, you've found Etienne to be arrogant and overbearing. Why the sudden change of heart?"

With a careless shrug, Ariane moved behind the chair and began to twist Marie-Claire's hair into a French plait. "Things change."

Cheeks puffed, Marie-Claire exhaled long and slow. "Um-hmm. Don't I know it."

"Are you going to be all right?"

"Eventually."

"Marie-Claire, I don't think Sebastian cares a fig for Veronike. After you left last night, he didn't speak a word to her.''

''Before he kissed her or after?''

Marie-Claire could fairly hear Ariane grimace. ''He *kissed* her?''

''On her big, bloated...bulbous...*bulging* lips.''

''*Really?*'' Surprised, Ariane stilled her hands and then she tut-tutted and once again began to weave her efficient braid. ''Well, it couldn't have been that great because every time I saw him, he was by himself and looking miserable. Eduardo on the other hand, mixed it up rather well on the dance floor with a number of young local ladies.''

Marie-Claire lifted her shoulder a notch. ''It doesn't matter. I've lost him.''

''Eduardo?'' Ariane tried to inject a little levity.

''Well, I've hurt him, too. I have a lot of apologizing to do.''

''When you do, you must bring me with you. Most of that kooky stuff was my idea.''

''But I was the one with the fruit on my head.''

''Yes, well, we all make mistakes. Especially when it comes to love.''

''Is that what you are doing now, by heading off to Rhineland?''

''Perhaps.'' Ariane secured Marie-Claire's braid with a clip and bent to kiss her cheek. ''Call me?''

''Mm-hmm. I'll be calling from Tatiana's house in Denmark. For some reason, when my life falls apart, she is the only one able to step in and mother me.''

''Give her my love.''

She covered Ariane's hand with her own. ''I will.''

As Marie-Claire watched her sister gather her belongings

and slip into the hall, she wondered listlessly at Ariane's sudden interest in Etienne Kroninberg, prince of Rhineland. For a while now, she'd noticed that Ariane had been acting rather more secretively than usual, and her motives for going to Rhineland were weak. After all, just six months ago Ariane seemed to have no feelings for Prince Etienne whatsoever. What had changed?

Fingertips wet from a touch to her tongue, Marie-Claire snuffed her candle, crawled into bed and assumed a fetal position. Her eyes drifted shut and she decided to worry about Ariane after she woke up.

Over a week later, Marie-Claire was just now able to lift her head from her pillow and venture out into the world again. She pulled her scarf more closely about her face and hunched against the blustery wind that nudged her down the busy streets of Copenhagen. Tatiana needed eggs and milk for a dessert she was making, hoping, no doubt, to put some weight on her granddaughter's skinny bones.

Marie-Claire snorted into the furry collar of her coat. Fat chance. Since she'd arrived in Denmark, she'd already lost five pounds. In all the wrong places. Story of her life.

Like a salmon fighting upstream, Marie-Claire navigated through the crowded sidewalk, faces coming, going, all strange, all a blur. Horns sounded, people shouted. Typical, these sounds of life in the city. Marie-Claire was glad for the anonymity. Being able to come and go without the intense scrutiny of the security guards was a rare and wonderful privilege.

As she drew near the market, she passed a newsstand and paused to catch up with life.

Her heart caught in her throat and her head began to buzz as she stared at the blaring headlines:

St. Michel's Royal Daughters Illegitimate?
Late King Philippe of St. Michel a Bigamist?

And even worse yet:

Sebastian LeMarc Crown Prince of St. Michel?

Clutching the sales table for balance, she perused the articles and her heart shifted from a dead standstill to overdrive. Icy with shock, Marie-Claire spun about and forced her legs to carry her all the way back to Tatiana's house, forgetting her errand in the process. She rushed inside, turned on the television and searched for a twenty-four-hour news station. After several misses, she hit upon the story being discussed on a Paris network.

"What is it, darling?" Concerned by Marie-Claire's frantic return and anxious demeanor, Tatiana moved from the kitchen to her parlor. She dusted her flour-coated hands on her apron, then perched on the couch beside Marie-Claire and adjusted her glasses.

"Listen, Tatiana. It's in the papers, too." Tears rose with the television's volume.

"—and this report is fueling further speculation about the sex of Queen Celeste's baby and whether this child will eventually take the throne.

"Recently, there has been speculation that Sebastian LeMarc, import/export mogul from St. Michel, is the missing heir apparent. However, Mr. LeMarc could not be reached for comment at this time. Palace officials in St. Michel also continue to have no comment, except to say that, quote, 'We are running the government smoothly and the people of St. Michel can be assured that when the crown prince comes to light, he will fit the DNA profile and all other criteria. These things take time. Speculation is not helpful at this juncture.' End quote.

"A reliable source close to the royal family does tell us that King Philippe married when he was only eighteen to an American named Katie Graham. The marriage was never annulled, making Philippe de Bergeron's subsequent marriages invalid, and his offspring illegitimate. And, in a related story, the government of Rhineland—"

Tatiana gasped. "Who would do such a thing?"

Remote in hand, Marie-Claire turned off the television and stared at the black screen, remembering what she'd just read in the paper.

"Wilhelm."

Luc Dumont heard the ring of his phone just as he was lathering his hair with shampoo. Typical. He slammed off the faucet and listened to the ring. Not his cell. Not the pager. Not the regular phone. Must be the fax. Good. He turned the water back on and ducked. The water sluiced over his head, hot and refreshing. He'd worked late last night at Interpol's satellite office in St. Michel and had used the better part of the wee hours researching the materials his men had spent this last week collecting on Claudette LeMarc and her late husband, Henri.

Seems that if there had been two sets of railroad tracks in St. Michel, Claudette would have been born on the wrong side of the wrong set. She'd grown up in abject poverty, her father a drunk and her mother bedridden after a stroke. Together, they'd had eight children, and Claudette, being the oldest, was no doubt expected to shoulder much of the parenting load.

A twinge of pity struck Luc as he lathered his body. If he had to guess, that was the reason Sebastian had no siblings. Claudette was tired of mothering by the time she got to him. Which raised several other good questions, including why she would bother to adopt so early in her marriage.

With both hands, Luc leaned against the fiberglass wall

and let the hot water pound on his back. Ah, well. The answers would surface all in good time. The pieces were certainly beginning to fall together.

Claudette had dropped out of school with a third-grade education and had met her husband Count Henri LeMarc in a pub where she worked as a cocktail waitress. His pedigree as a descendent of a twelfth-century line of French aristocrats, had impressed her and they were married just four weeks later. Sebastian was born in a hospital in northern France nine months after that.

Once again, Luc shut off the water and, grabbing a towel, mopped himself off and tied it around his hips. He moved to the fax machine, picked up the sheet that had fallen to the floor and began to read. Finally. The DNA test results had arrived at the French offices of Interpol that morning. And, as he flipped through the subsequent pages, he realized with a start that Sebastian LeMarc's fate had been sealed.

Tatiana Van Rhys had always been a rebel. Photos of herself and her young daughter, Johanna, were scattered around her living room, always depicting them doing something adventurous. One photo was of them sky-diving. Another of them mountain-climbing. And yet another of them smiling on a sailboat, holding up fish nearly as large as they were. On the end table beside the couch where Marie-Claire sat was a particularly beautiful picture of Johanna skiing in the Swiss Alps.

Marie-Claire peered closely at her mother's blissful smile and felt stirrings of melancholy for that mother-daughter relationship. Now, more than ever, she needed her mother, even though Johanna had never really had a maternal bone in her body.

Rebellion seemed to run in the family, Marie-Claire thought wryly, as she regarded her grandmother's simple cottage. Having lived her entire married life in a palace, Tatiana, as a widow, now preferred this simplicity and the freedom that came with it.

Outside the curtained windows a March wind blustered, but inside by the fire, it was cozy. Safe from the injustices of life. The small living room was tidy and furnished with odds and ends and souvenirs of Tatiana's many travels and the kitchen always had the smell of something freshly baked, as it did now.

Marie-Claire could see Tatiana withdrawing Danish pastries from the oven and drizzling icing on them. The kettle whistled and cups clanked. Upon her arrival in Denmark this last time, Marie-Claire had decided never again to leave this homey haven, especially since there was no real reason to return to St. Michel anymore. She'd stay here and take care of Tatiana, when and if the tiny dynamo ever needed caretaking, and then, when Tatiana passed on, she would be the next old lady to love this house.

Fragrant tray in hand, Tatiana swept into the room and pressing an ottoman into service as a table, poured them each a cup of tea. Gooey and warm, the Danish would tide them over until suppertime. All afternoon, she and her grandmother had been deep in a conversation that had Marie-Claire regaling a softly clucking Tatiana with the details of Philippe's secret marriage that, until now, had been known only to Simone.

"—and he was three years younger than I am now. Can you believe that? I guess, when they found out she was going to have a baby they ran away to France to get married. They were very brave, I think, to buck convention and marry."

Tatiana had held her tongue for the better part of an hour, which for her, was a minor miracle. But now, she had to unleash her opinions or burst.

"Child, do you want to live your life with a man you do not love?"

"What? No."

"Well, that's just what your mother did, poor thing. And I was partly responsible. I encouraged the marriage between your mother and father, because my husband—God rest his soul—convinced me that it would be a good political alliance. But from the minute your mother said 'I do,' I could see that the child was miserable. I have always carried a terrible load of guilt over that. She was never cut out to be a wife. Or, unfortunately for you lovely girls, a mother. But thank God she had you, no?"

Marie-Claire swallowed hard and nodded.

"Even so, I can never encourage anyone not to follow their heart again."

"But Sebastian is convinced that he is my brother."

"Stuff and nonsense. You have a very good feel for character, my child. If your gut tells you that Claudette is lying, then I don't doubt that she is. From everything you've told me so far, it would only stand to reason."

Marie-Claire set down her teacup then flopped back and rolled her head toward Tatiana. "Thank you for your vote of confidence, Grandmama, but last time I saw Sebastian, he was lip-locked with Veronike Schroeder."

"I'm going to hazard a guess that he kissed her for a very good reason."

"Which is?"

"Why, how better to protect you from the unknown? My darling, if he were to have thrown caution to the wind and declared his undying love to the public that night, where do you think you and he would be right now?"

Marie-Claire gestured limply at the television. "On that show?"

"Precisely. Now, my sweet, as much as I hate to do this,

I'm going to kick you out of my house. I want you to go home and get to the bottom of this. Certainly, the truth will surface soon. And, when it does, you need to be there to fight for your man.''

Sebastian was fighting mad. Blood pumping like the bellows that fanned the flames of hell, he stared at the papers Simone had just faxed to him at Claudette's house. He could taste murder in the bile that rose in his throat as he swung around to face her. His mother cowered in the corner. He advanced on her, brandishing the faxed papers.

"Why?" he shouted.

"Why...what?" Claudette cringed more deeply into her calfskin club chair.

"Don't play dumb with me, Mère. I have papers here that spell out the unfortunate fact that I am indeed your flesh and blood. Though it seems that we are both reluctant to admit that.''

"What is that you have there?" Holding out one last hope that her dreams of becoming the next dowager queen were not crashing down around her, Claudette gestured to the pages he held.

"This is news from Interpol in France. DNA results that state unequivocally that thirty-two years ago, in a hospital in France, the woman who bore me, was you. Claudette Alexandra LeMarc. Not Katie Graham, in some tragic story that you concocted.''

Now that Sebastian knew the truth, Claudette shifted into an offensive mode and sitting up straight, did her best to smoothly backpedal. "Sebastian, surely you could not have learned to be such an ingrate from me! I did all of this *for you*. In your best interests.''

Jaw slack, Sebastian stared at this illogical woman he once thought he knew. "You think that *lying* about my parentage and slipping me into the royal family like some...*cuckoo's egg,* was in my best interest?'' Sebastian advanced to the edge of her chair and, gripping the edge until the wood frame cracked, leaned down. His voice was low. Menacing. Deadly. ''What kind of crazy are you?''

Hand to throat, Claudette leaned away from him, afraid. ''I thought that after you were in place, all the questions would die down. They would see, as I do, that you are the one who should wield the power in this country. You would make a wonderful king.''

''Not if I am not *born to the position!*'' Sebastian strode several paces away from her. ''Do you realize what you have cost me? Do you have any idea at all, what your self-ishness has done?''

Her stare was blank.

''No. I see that you do not. Mère—'' Nose to nose again, Sebastian inclined his head to the mass of clutter in her parlor. ''It is time for you to grow up. I have just two suggestions for you. First, you need to take back everything you have purchased in the last month, and then have an estate sale and get rid of everything else. When you have finished that gargantuan task, I suggest,'' his gaze stabbed into hers, ''that you get a job.''

''A...'' Claudette looked as if she'd just swallowed something rancid, ''a job?''

''If you wish to continue eating, yes.'' Sebastian pushed off her chair, reached for his overcoat and tossed it over his shoulder. ''I'm going to the palace to beg forgiveness for your temporary insanity. I'll tell Simone to expect you soon so that you can do the same. Then, if she can even still look me in the eye, I'm going to ask for her granddaughter's hand in marriage.''

Forgetting the hot water within which she was boiling, Claudette leapt to her feet and clasped her hands in a rapturous manner. "You will be joining the royal family after all?"

"If I am lucky, yes, I'll be joining the royal family. You, on the other hand, will be joining the work force. Good luck, Mère."

Once back at home in St. Michel, Marie-Claire was anxious to discuss the headlines she'd seen with Luc Dumont. After stowing her bags in her suite, she was told he was in one of the palace's comfortable salons. She found him sitting with the dowager queen, flustered over some sharp remark the old woman had just made. Upon spotting Marie-Claire, Simone beckoned. "Come here, darling girl, and save me from this boy's endless flirtation."

Flushing crimson, Luc opened his mouth to protest but thinking better, instead heaved a resigned sigh.

Simone ignored him. "How was your trip to Copenhagen?"

Marie-Claire grinned in sympathy at Luc, then turned to Simone.

"I heard the news. Saw it in the papers, even there."

"I was hoping we could spare the world our dirty laundry, but Wilhelm—" Simone's eyes clouded over and she swallowed hard.

"I know. How is Lise holding up?"

"As can be expected. Depressed about Wilhelm. Morning sick with the baby. Still grieving Philippe. Trying to cope with possible illegitimacy. Other than that, she's in fine fettle."

"I'll go see her in a moment. But first, I heard that the palace is still officially denying Sebastian as crown prince. What are we waiting for?"

"You haven't heard? Oh, darling, I'm so thoughtless. I should have called you first! Luc here has discovered through a series of DNA tests, that there is no way that Sebastian is Philippe's son.''

''What?'' Marie-Claire whispered as joy surged into her throat.

''Yes, it seems that Claudette was lying to save her spendthrift hide. Although I forgave her and assigned her a job in the palace kitchen, slicing onions. Which reminds me. I must check on her now.'' Before she could struggle to her feet, Luc leapt to assist. ''I'm too old for you, son,'' she groused and slapped his hand from her arm.

''But—''

''Why don't you focus this energy on someone your own age. Tell this child about Claudette's deception and leave me be. Marie-Claire, you can ask him the finer points of the case, but suffice it to say, we are still searching for the crown prince.''

Relief lifted her out of her chair and Marie-Claire stood watching her grandmother totter out of the room. ''She's a tease,'' Marie-Claire said once her grandmother was out of earshot.

''I'm finding that out.''

Hands clasped under her chin, Marie-Claire looked deeply into Luc's eyes. ''So it's true. Sebastian is not my brother.''

''No. In fact, I'm in the process of tracing Katie Graham's marriage certificate to Texas. So we're back to the drawing board.''

Laughing, Marie-Claire rushed forward and, grabbing him round the neck, stood on tiptoe and soundly kissed his cheeks. Pleased, he made no effort to back away.

''Oh,'' she breathed, ''thank you, thank you!''

''My pleasure. Anything else I can do?''

''Yes. You can let her go.'' Sebastian's voice, like the voice of an angry mythical god boomed fire from behind them and before they could even protest, he'd grabbed Luc by the scruff of the neck and landed a neat right cross to his face.

Surprised, Luc reeled, and falling to the floor, clutched the welt that was forming at his jaw. "What the *hell?*"

Astonished, Marie-Claire emitted a strangled scream. *"Sebastian!"*

"This time," Sebastian roared, "I'm not getting hit." He dove down and lifted Luc off the floor by his shirt. Luc dangled, still too shocked to register the fact that Sebastian LeMarc was preparing to beat him to a bloody pulp.

"Sebastian," Marie-Claire rushed to grab his arm, "stop it! Luc is simply telling me the truth! That you are not the crown prince! That you are not my brother! That we can," she burst into tears, "be together."

Sebastian dropped Luc with a thud.

"For crying out loud," Luc moaned from the floor, "what is it with this family?" Dragging himself to his feet, Luc stood swaying and pointed at them. "I keep getting accused of flirting and dammit, *I'm not!*" With that, he straightened his shirt and staggered out of the room.

"Dumont," Sebastian called after him, "I'm really sorry—"

Luc waved a hand behind him. "Yeah, yeah," he muttered and left.

Slowly, Sebastian turned and stood, watching Marie-Claire, and she was reminded of that night at the pond, when his eyes saw into her soul. His hands settled at his narrow hips, and, breathing hard, she thought how masculine he was, always charging in to save her from herself.

"So you know." Boyishly, he pushed the fingertips of one hand through his hair, straightening it.

"Yes." Marie-Claire nodded, her pulse drumming crazily, and she fought the urge to move to him and tousle his hair.

"You were right."

"You will have to learn to live with that, as I usually am."

Sebastian rolled his eyes.

A slow smile tugged at the corners of her mouth.

They stood, transfixed with helpless wonder at their sudden freedom.

"Come here," he whispered.

Marie-Claire need not be told twice. She ran the few steps it took to fling herself into his powerful arms and fill her hands with his hair.

Noses bumped, chins collided, but it only took an instant for their mouths to come home. Marie-Claire's laughter turned to a liquid moan as he gave her the kiss she'd been wanting for weeks. Wilting in his arms, she could feel her heartbeat pounding against his and hear his breath coming in labored pants.

"Ahh, Marie-Claire," he whispered. "How I've missed you."

"Mmm." He swallowed her heartfelt reply.

How long they stood like this was anybody's guess, but the clock chimed the quarter and half hours. The kisses ebbed and flowed, entwined with whispered endearments, ripening to perfection like fine wine. Marie-Claire draped her arms over his shoulders and fell back, dangling in his embrace, loving the onslaught.

"I missed this."

"Yes," she murmured.

"You have certainly helped me realize three very important things in this life."

"Mmm. And what would they be?"

"Well, for one thing, that life is very short, and to waste even a moment is a sin."

Her head snapped up and her eyes flew to his. "That's just what I learned from you!"

"Ahh, good. Then you won't refuse me, when I ask you to mar—"

"Yes!" Marie-Claire's squeal was gleeful as she pulled his face low for another kiss.

"I don't want to wait," Sebastian said, when she let him up for air.

"Neither do I."

"Good. You have two weeks."

"Two weeks?"

"Just enough time to let the public digest the fact that we are not related. Yet, anyway."

Marie-Claire nodded, the cogs in her mind already grinding into motion. "Two weeks is not much time, but I'm up to the task. There are cable shows and advice columns dealing with just such emergencies...."

"God help us all," Sebastian moaned.

Marie-Claire giggled and buried her fingers into his back pants pockets. "Sebastian?"

"Hmm?" He was busy kissing the back of her jaw, directly under her ear.

"What else have you realized?"

"Uh...I forgot."

Her laughter was lazy. "You did not. Think."

"I can't."

"Tell me."

Eyes heavy with desire, Sebastian paused and thought. "Oh. The second thing is that I have no desire ever to live above my means. So. If you'll agree to live with me at my house in the—"

"Yes!" Again, Marie-Claire cut him off with a long, soulful kiss.

"And last, but certainly most important of all, I love you more than any man has ever loved a woman."

"Oh, Sebastian. I love you."

Sebastian loosened his collar. "You know, it's still going to take some adjusting, to get me over the idea that you are not my sister."

Marie-Claire growled and tugged his lower lip between her teeth.

"Okay. I'm adjusted," he said, and angled her mouth beneath his.

Epilogue

Through a wide arched doorway made of stone, an ethereal gold light, courtesy of the setting sun, streamed into a small garden niche. Just outside the palace walls, it housed a large glass gazebo, erected just for this special occasion. The site was perfect for a twilight wedding in the middle of April.

Fragrance from the spring flowers that crowded the formal gardens wafted about on the light breezes and into the open windows. Gentle spring rains misted the leaded panes on the roof, refracting light and dazzling the guests. Peastone paths wended through pine trees and thickly flowered rhododendron bushes and bulbs of hyacinth and tulip, all culminating at the arched door.

Inside the glass house, candles burned and light harpsichord music played as Marie-Claire moved, escorted by a smiling prime minister, toward Sebastian. Made of French silk and Italian chiffon, Marie-Claire's dress swished along the satin floor runner and Sebastian thought he'd never seen anything so beautiful in his life.

The audience was small, only Marie-Claire's family and

a few friends. A much chastened Claudette sat in the front row, crying real tears at the beauty of the occasion. Ariane had flown home from Rhineland for the ceremony and stood with Lise as maid and matron of honor.

As all weddings do, this one moved to its swift conclusion with an exchange of vows and a kiss that lingered nearly as long as the ceremony had. The minister, having pronounced them husband and wife, held up his hands to still the applause.

"Ladies and gentlemen, it is my privilege, for the first time ever, to introduce Mr. and Mrs. Sebastian LeMarc."

Over the din, Sebastian leaned in to better hear Marie-Claire.

"So," she said, "we are family after all."

He nodded and whispered back. "So we are, my wife. But our family is way too small, to my way of thinking."

"Are you suggesting that we skip the reception?"

"If we leave now, we can be starting on that baby in less than an hour."

Losing a slipper as she went, Marie-Claire grabbed his hand and together, they ran into happily ever after.

*   *   *   *   *

*Turn the page for a sneak preview
of the next* ROYALLY WED:
THE MISSING HEIR *title,*

IN PURSUIT OF A PRINCESS

*Etienne and Ariane's story!
by Donna Clayton
on sale in April 2002 in
Silhouette Romance...*

*And don't miss any of the books in the
Royally Wed series,
only from Silhouette Romance:*

*OF ROYAL BLOOD, March 2002
by Carolyn Zane*

*IN PURSUIT OF A PRINCESS,
April 2002
by Donna Clayton*

*A PRINCESS IN WAITING, May 2002
by Carol Grace*

*A PRINCE AT LAST!, June 2002
by Cathie Linz*

Chapter One

Prince Etienne Kroninberg of Rhineland slipped into the ballroom using a side door. His parents would have his head for being late. But the matter couldn't be helped, he thought. He could only meet with the most trusted members of his Intelligence Service when everyone else was otherwise occupied.

Ruthless rumors were afloat. It had been reported to him that a person—or persons—within his father's cabinet wanted to seize control of the neighboring country of St. Michel. Etienne was appalled that someone wanted to take advantage of the de Bergeron family when they were still in mourning over the loss of King Philippe. The idea was barbaric in this day and age.

Granted, the unexpected death of the king left the country with no male heir—and it was common knowledge that the law of St. Michel declared that females could not rule. It was an archaic edict, but legally enforceable, nonetheless. No war would be fought. Not a single Rhineland soldier would march across St. Michel's border. This battle would be waged in the international courts. And all of this would take place in a civilized and peaceful manner. Yet it would be nonetheless barbaric in Etienne's mind.

He let his gaze travel slowly over the guests in the ballroom. It took but an instant to find who he was looking for. She stood out in the crowd, his princess did. Ariane was that stunning. Heat spiraled like liquid smoke low in his gut.

Her honey-blond hair was twisted into an intricate coiffure, a few loose and softly curly strands falling to brush against her sexy bare shoulders whenever she moved her head. The line of her milky neck was long and graceful and delicate. She had the kind of throat that enticed a man to press his nose against warm skin, to inhale the distinct and subtle womanly aroma that would be hers and hers alone. Ariane, he silently surmised, would smell of sunny summer days and flowery meadows.

He had to admit, Princess Ariane's visit had him more than a bit perplexed. He'd made his intentions known prior to her father's passing. King Philippe had let Etienne know that he was quite in favor of a match between himself and Ariane. Etienne's own father was in favor of such an alliance as well. However, Princess Ariane hadn't seemed the least interested in Etienne as a suitor.

No one had been more surprised than Etienne when the de Bergeron royal envoy had arrived announcing Princess Ariane's intentions of visiting Rhineland.

He started across the floor. Surely, the Princess would be feeling affronted by his tardiness. He had some groveling to do. He may as well get it over with.

When he approached, all conversation stopped.

"Your Highness." He bowed low, wanting to express his profound apology. He straightened, leveling his gaze on her beautiful deep-blue eyes. "Please forgive me." He pressed a light kiss, first to one cheek, then the other, taking full advantage of the old-style traditional greeting. Her skin was warm satin against his lips. "I hope you believe me when I say my late arrival couldn't be avoided. I do apologize for my absence."

He'd been wrong. Her scent didn't bring to mind summer days and wildflowers. She smelled of starlit nights washed clean by fresh rain.

Her lovely gaze went round and she said, "You've been absent?"

The two men standing in the small group did their best to stifle the humor incited by the Princess's cutting question.

Touché, Etienne thought. He deserved that. She had every right to put him in his place.

Her smile was dazzling enough to steal away a man's thoughts.

"I've been having a wonderful conversation with the reverends here," she told him.

What she'd said took him aback. Surely the lords had introduced themselves. Unable to quell his surprise, he queried, "Reverends?"

"Yes," she said. "The pastors here were just telling me about your beautiful country."

"Princess," Etienne felt compelled to correct, "Lord Hecht is Minister of the Interior. One of his many duties includes suggesting policy for our parklands." The man named Hecht offered Ariane an indulgent smile. "And Lord Bartelow is Deputy Minister of Trade. He advises the king on issues of commerce." When Ariane's gaze still didn't seem to register understanding, he allowed himself to go a little further. "These men have been appointed by my father to help him run our government."

Ariane's chuckle sounded like tiny bells as she focused her attention on the two elderly men. "Oh...and here I thought I'd been talking to men of the cloth. I heard the word *minister* and...well, I just naturally assumed..."

Again, she laughed. Daintily. Infectiously. And although the lords politely joined her, Etienne could tell from the quick, covert expressions that passed between them what they were thinking: if brain cells were dynamite, the lovely princess apparently wouldn't have enough to blow her nose.

This exchange was Etienne's first inkling that something about the de Bergeron princess seemed...well, shifted just a little bit left of center. Her behavior was somehow...off. And as he stood there listening to her talk, this deviation from what he thought should be the norm became more and more pronounced. He wasn't too proud to admit that the situation had him highly perplexed.

As the evening progressed, Etienne became downright amazed at how the princess would ask seemingly coherent questions regarding someone's political position only to make a frivolous comment that left her looking, well, less than intelligent.

Etienne honestly didn't know what to think. Maybe Ariane wasn't the woman he'd believed her to be.

From what he'd learned of Ariane de Bergeron, he'd had high hopes that she could very well be the perfect woman for him. Sources had informed him that the princess had a head on her shoulders...a head supposedly filled with an impressive brain. However, if he were to believe what he was seeing—and hearing—this evening he'd have to say there was nothing more than a big air bubble between her ears.

"She's perfect," he said softly, repeating his father's opinion.

Self-assured, humorous, well-educated. The description haunted Etienne's mind.

Something wasn't right here. All the information he'd

been given pointed out the fact that things were not adding up. Ariane *was* all of those things, Etienne was sure. And if he was sure of that, then her behavior had to be some sort of put-on.

He sighed. But that just made no sense to him. No sense at all.

However, for some odd reason, it seemed as though the princess wanted the people of his country to think she was naive and…well, dim-witted. She was putting on a show. And quite a show it was, at that.

But the question was…for whom? And why?

*   *   *   *   *

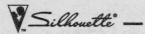

Silhouette®

where love comes alive—online...

eHARLEQUIN.com

your romantic
books

- ♥ **Shop online!** Visit Shop eHarlequin and discover a wide selection of new releases and classic favorites at great discounted prices.

- ♥ Read our daily and weekly Internet exclusive serials, and participate in our interactive novel in the reading room.

- ♥ Ever dreamed of being a writer? Enter your chapter for a chance to become a featured author in our Writing Round Robin novel.

your romantic
magazine

- ♥ Check out our feature articles on dating, flirting and other important romance topics and get your daily love dose with tips on how to keep the romance alive every day.

- ♥ Learn what the stars have in store for you with our daily Passionscopes and weekly Erotiscopes.

- ♥ Get the latest scoop on your favorite royals in Royal Romance.

your
community

- ♥ Have a Heart-to-Heart with other members about the latest books and meet your favorite authors.

- ♥ Discuss your romantic dilemma in the Tales from the Heart message board.

All this and more available at
www.eHarlequin.com

SINTA1R2

This Mother's Day
Give Your Mom
 A Royal Treat

Win a fabulous one-week vacation in
Puerto Rico for you and your mother at
the luxurious Inter-Continental San Juan
Resort & Casino. The prize includes round
trip airfare for two, breakfast daily and a
mother and daughter day of beauty
at the beachfront hotel's spa.

INTER·CONTINENTAL
San Juan
RESORT & CASINO

Here's all you have to do:

Tell us in 100 words or less how your
mother helped with the romance in your
life. It may be a story about your engagement,
wedding or those boyfriends when you were
a teenager or any other romantic advice
from your mother. The entry will be judged
based on its originality, emotionally
compelling nature and sincerity.
See official rules on following page.

Send your entry to:
Mother's Day Contest

In Canada
P.O. Box 637
Fort Erie, Ontario
L2A 5X3

In U.S.A.
P.O. Box 9076
3010 Walden Ave.
Buffalo, NY
14269-9076

Or enter online at www.eHarlequin.com

PRROY

HARLEQUIN MOTHER'S DAY CONTEST 2216
OFFICIAL RULES
NO PURCHASE NECESSARY TO ENTER

Two ways to enter:

• **Via The Internet:** Log on to the Harlequin romance website (www.eHarlequin.com) anytime beginning 12:01 a.m. E.S.T., January 1, 2002 through 11:59 p.m. E.S.T., April 1, 2002 and follow the directions displayed on-line to enter your name, address (including zip code), e-mail address and in 100 words or fewer, describe how your mother helped with the romance in your life.

• **Via Mail:** Handprint (or type) on an 8 1/2" x 11" plain sheet of paper, your name, address (including zip code) and e-mail address (if you have one), and in 100 words or fewer, describe how your mother helped with the romance in your life. Mail your entry via first-class mail to: Harlequin Mother's Day Contest 2216, (in the U.S.) P.O. Box 9076, Buffalo, NY 14269-9076; (in Canada) P.O. Box 637, Fort Erie, Ontario, Canada L2A 5X3.

For eligibility, entries must be submitted either through a completed Internet transmission or postmarked no later than 11:59 p.m. E.S.T., April 1, 2002 (mail-in entries must be received by April 9, 2002). Limit one entry per person, household address and e-mail address. On-line and/or mailed entries received from persons residing in geographic areas in which entry is not permissible will be disqualified.

Entries will be judged by a panel of judges, consisting of members of the Harlequin editorial, marketing and public relations staff using the following criteria:
  • Originality - 50%
  • Emotional Appeal - 25%
  • Sincerity - 25%

In the event of a tie, duplicate prizes will be awarded. Decisions of the judges are final.

Prize: A 6-night/7-day stay for two at the Inter-Continental San Juan Resort & Casino, including round-trip coach air transportation from gateway airport nearest winner's home (approximate retail value: $4,000). Prize includes breakfast daily and a mother and daughter day of beauty at the beachfront hotel's spa. Prize consists of only those items listed as part of the prize. Prize is valued in U.S. currency.

All entries become the property of Torstar Corp. and will not be returned. No responsibility is assumed for lost, late, illegible, incomplete, inaccurate, non-delivered or misdirected mail or misdirected e-mail, for technical, hardware or software failures of any kind, lost or unavailable network connections, or failed, incomplete, garbled or delayed computer transmission or any human error which may occur in the receipt or processing of the entries in this Contest.

Contest open only to residents of the U.S. (except Colorado) and Canada, who are 18 years of age or older and is void wherever prohibited by law; all applicable laws and regulations apply. Any litigation within the Province of Quebec respecting the conduct or organization of a publicity contest may be submitted to the Régie des alcools, des courses et des jeux for a ruling. Any litigation respecting the awarding of a prize may be submitted to the Régie des alcools, des courses et des jeux only for the purpose of helping the parties reach a settlement. Employees and immediate family members of Torstar Corp. and D.L. Blair, Inc., their affiliates, subsidiaries and all other agencies, entities and persons connected with the use, marketing or conduct of this Contest are not eligible to enter. Taxes on prize are the sole responsibility of winner. Acceptance of any prize offered constitutes permission to use winner's name, photograph or other likeness for the purposes of advertising, trade and promotion on behalf of Torstar Corp., its affiliates and subsidiaries without further compensation to the winner, unless prohibited by law.

Winner will be determined no later than April 15, 2002 and be notified by mail. Winner will be required to sign and return an Affidavit of Eligibility form within 15 days after winner notification. Non-compliance within that time period may result in disqualification and an alternate winner may be selected. Winner of trip must execute a Release of Liability prior to ticketing and must possess required travel documents (e.g. Passport, photo ID) where applicable. Travel must be completed within 12 months of selection and is subject to traveling companion completing and returning a Release of Liability prior to travel; and hotel and flight accommodations availability. Certain restrictions and blackout dates may apply. No substitution of prize permitted by winner. Torstar Corp. and D.L. Blair, Inc., their parents, affiliates, and subsidiaries are not responsible for errors in printing or electronic presentation of Contest, or entries. In the event of printing or other errors which may result in unintended prize values or duplication of prizes, all affected entries shall be null and void. If for any reason the Internet portion of the Contest is not capable of running as planned, including infection by computer virus, bugs, tampering, unauthorized intervention, fraud, technical failures, or any other causes beyond the control of Torstar Corp. which corrupt or affect the administration, secrecy, fairness, integrity or proper conduct of the Contest, Torstar Corp. reserves the right, at its sole discretion, to disqualify any individual who tampers with the entry process and to cancel, terminate, modify or suspend the Contest or the Internet portion thereof. In the event the Internet portion must be terminated a notice will be posted on the website and all entries received prior to termination will be judged in accordance with these rules. In the event of a dispute regarding an on-line entry, the entry will be deemed submitted by the authorized holder of the e-mail account submitted at the time of entry. Authorized account holder is defined as the natural person who is assigned to an e-mail address by an Internet access provider, on-line service provider or other organization that is responsible for arranging e-mail address for the domain associated with the submitted e-mail address. Torstar Corp. and/or D.L. Blair Inc. assumes no responsibility for any computer injury or damage related to or resulting from accessing and/or downloading any sweepstakes material. Rules are subject to any requirements/limitations imposed by the FCC. Purchase or acceptance of a product offer does not improve your chances of winning.

For winner's name (available after May 1, 2002), send a self-addressed, stamped envelope to: Harlequin Mother's Day Contest Winners 2216, P.O. Box 4200 Blair, NE 68009-4200 or you may access the www.eHarlequin.com Web site through June 3, 2002.

Contest sponsored by Torstar Corp., P.O. Box 9042, Buffalo, NY 14269-9042.